A Gangster's Code

Lock Down Publications and
Ca$h Presents
A Gangster's Code
A Novel by **J-Blunt**

A GANGSTER'S CODE

Lock Down Publications
P.O. Box 870494
Mesquite, Tx 75187

Visit our website
www.lockdownpublications.com

Copyright 2018 by A Gangster's Code

All rights reserved. No part of this book may be reproduced in any form or by electronic or mechanical means, including information storage and retrieval systems without permission in writing from the publisher, except by a reviewer who may quote brief passages in review.
First Edition August 2018
Printed in the United States of America

This is a work of fiction. Names, characters, places, and incidents either are products of the author's imagination or are used fictitiously. Any similarity to actual events or locales or persons, living or dead, is entirely coincidental.

Lock Down Publications
Like our page on Facebook: Lock Down Publications @
www.facebook.com/lockdownpublications.ldp
Cover design and layout by: **Dynasty Cover Me**
Book interior design by: **Shawn Walker**
Edited by: **Lauren Burton**

Stay Connected with Us!

Text **LOCKDOWN** to 22828 to stay up-to-date with new releases, sneak peeks, contests and more…

Submission Guideline.

Submit the first three chapters of your completed manuscript to ldpsubmissions@gmail.com, subject line: Your book's title. The manuscript must be in a .doc file and sent as an attachment. The document should be in Times New Roman, double-spaced and in size 12 font. Also, provide your synopsis and full contact information. If sending multiple submissions, they must each be in a separate email.

Have a story but no way to send it electronically? You can still submit to LDP/Ca$h Presents. Send in the first three chapters, written or typed, of your completed manuscript to:

LDP: Submissions Dept
Po Box 870494
Mesquite, Tx 75187

DO NOT send original manuscript. Must be a duplicate.

Provide your synopsis and a cover letter containing your full contact information.

Thanks for considering LDP and Ca$h Presents.

J-BLUNT

A GANGSTER'S CODE

Prologue

The ghetto was alive: loud music, cars on chrome rims, females walking around in tight clothing, and niggas standing on porches trying to holla. The atmosphere changed when the white Lexus turned onto the block. A hush came over the hood as all eyes flocked to the car. It pulled to a stop in front of a house in the middle of the block. Two people were inside, a man in the driver's seat and a female in the passenger's.

"What I tell you 'bout that boyfriend shit? Let me catch you fuckin' wit' one of these bitch-ass niggas and I'ma body his ass."

"C'mon, cousin. I'm sixteen. When you was sixteen you had a girlfriend. Why can't I have a boyfriend?"

"'Cause niggas ain't shit."

"What about you?"

He paused. "I ain't shit, either."

"But if it wasn't for you, we wouldn't have a place to live. I know everybody scared of you, but I love you. What if I get a boyfriend like you?"

"No boys, Shanice! I ain't playin'. I don't care what cho momma say. Now, take this money and get out. I got some shit to do."

After a hug, Shanice took the five hundred dollars and got out of the car. Before closing the door, she spun around. "Paul, do you think –"

"Aye! What I tell you 'bout that shit? Don't call me Paul no more!"

"Sorry. Pop Somethin', do you think –"

Bocca! Bocca! Bocca! Bocca! Bocca!

Bullets tore through the Lexus' tinted windows, one of them hitting Pop Somethin' in the shoulder. He ducked, grabbing the Uzi from his lap.

"Shanice, run!"

The fully automatic machinegun bullets tore out the rest of the window as he fired the gun blindly at his attackers. More gunfire was exchanged as the luxury car sped away.

"Bitch-ass niggas!" Pop Somethin' cursed, the burning in his shoulder getting worse.

Pop-pop-pop-pop-pop-pop!

The Lexus' rear window smashed as bullets tore through the car. A black Infinity was chasing the Lexus. Someone was hanging out of the passenger's window, shooting wildly.

"Oh, you niggas want drama!" Pop yelled, smashing the brakes and bringing the Lexus to a sliding stop. He jumped out of the car with his finger holding the Uzi's trigger. The fully automatic sprayed bullets across the Infinity's windshield, tearing into the driver's face, neck, and chest. The black coupe swerved and crashed into a parked car. Pop knew whoever was in the car was in bad shape. He wanted to finish the kill, but his hurting shoulder and sirens in the background made him move back toward the Lexus.

Pop-pop-pop-pop-pop-pop!

A burning pain hit him in the back. His legs gave out and he fell to the ground. Pop tried to get up, but couldn't. He could feel the blood pouring from his wounds, then blackness.

Chapter 1

Eight years later

"C'mon, nigga. It's yo' move. Hurry up."

The big man ignored his friend's prompting, taking his time like he always did. He combed long fingers through his thick beard, fully lost in thought. When one of his shoulder-length dreadlocks slipped into his face, he threw his head back, shaking his mane like a lion until he got the wild hair under control. When satisfied, Pop Somethin' continued studying the chessboard. If he didn't make the right move, it would be his last move, and he couldn't let that happen. He ran the yard on the chessboard. B-Dog couldn't win. Nobody had jackin' rights on Pop Somethin'. Nobody.

"You see how he stallin' me out, Old School?" B-Dog asked an older convict who stood around watching the game.

"Chess is a thinking man's game, B-Dog. A strategic war game. You know Pop Somethin' is a war general. Give him time to think. I got a box of soups that says Pop Somethin' comes back and wins."

"Keep yo' money, Old School. I don't like takin' from my elders," B-Dog laughed.

Pop Somethin' finally made his move. "Three moves to mate."

B-Dog studied the board. He didn't see what Pop Somethin' was talking about. "Yeah right, nigga. You finna lose. Old School, we on for them soups. Fuck it. I got a few hungry niggas on the team that need to eat."

B-Dog made a move. Pop followed.

"Aye, y'all. Look." TK said, looking across the yard.

Four men moved quickly across the rec field with serious looks on their faces. These weren't average inmates. They were huge, looked like they ate the weights after they lifted them. They were known as ABK: Anybody Killas. They took what they wanted and preyed on the weak. In their line of sight were two squares slipping with their backs turned.

"Fool an' 'em stay on that bullshit," B-Dog laughed.

Pop Somethin' stood to his feet, tying his long dreads into a ponytail. "Them niggas some bitches."

"Nigga, whatchu doin'?" B-Dog asked.

"Them niggas tried that same shit wit' me when I first got here. Fuck ABK. I hate bitch-ass niggas. I told Buck Wild I was gon' be on his ass from there on out."

"C'mon, Pop. You finna go home in six months. You know what them niggas do ain't got shit to do wit' us."

"Yeah, it do. He know them lame-ass niggas ain't gon' fight back. They don't do them white boys like that 'cause they know them Aryans'll be on they ass. I ain't finna let 'em do fool an' 'em like that."

B-Dog stood with his nigga. "Damn, Pop. You always gettin' us in some bullshit."

***

The ABKs moved fast, surrounding the two squares. The short, light-skinned nigga trembled as Buck Wild spoke. "Where that bag at, C-Note? I heard you went on a visit yesterday. Where my shit?"

"C'mon, Buck. I gotta eat, my nigga. I'ma hit chu later. I thought we was good. I just hit yo' hand last week."

"Nah, nigga. It don't work like that. When you eat, I eat. I got a team to feed. Where my cut?"

"C'mon, Buck! Damn, man!" C-Note whined.

"You sound like a bitch, nigga. Gimme my shit 'fore I get in yo' ass and take the whole pack. See, my goons ready to bleed yo' ass."

C-Note looked from Buck Wild to his boys. They wore mean mugs and flexed their muscles, ready to do damage as soon as Buck gave the word. C-Note knew they would break his bones if he didn't give them what they wanted. He was about to dig in his underwear for the pack when another group approached.

"Whatchu doin', Buck?"

Buck Wild spun around, mugging Pop Somethin' and his boys. The ABKs were big and intimidating, and so was Pop and his niggas. Pop Somethin' stood six-foot-six and weighed 240 pounds. B-Dog was six foot and 200 pounds. TK was six-foot-nine and 260 pounds. All of them were chiseled from gruesome workouts led by Pop Somethin'.

"Get out my bidness, Pop," Buck mugged.

"You fuckin' in my bidness. You takin' food from my squad. I can't let that happen."

Buck laughed. "Take that cape off, nigga. Me and C-Note got an agreement. Ain't that right?"

Everybody looked to C-Note, waiting on his answer, but he was stuck. ABKs were beasts. They wrecked shit and spilled blood if a nigga looked at them wrong, but Pop Somethin' was a legend on the streets and in the joint. Nobody fucked with Pop Somethin' unless they had a death wish.

"You ain't gotta answer that, li'l bruh," Pop Somethin' spoke up. "Whatever deal y'all had is canceled. I got a better one. Lemme holla at chu."

C-Note made up his mind and walked toward Pop Somethin'. One of the ABKs grabbed him by the neck and threw him against the wall. TK moved like he was going to help, and one of the ABKs upped a shank. As soon as Pop Somethin' seen the knife, he punched Buck in the jaw, then it went up. Buck and Pop exchanged blows, neither of them ducking or dodging. It was a slugfest. They stood toe-to-toe and dropped bombs. TK pulled his own shank, him and the ABK dancing in a circle, taking knife swings at each other. B-Dog fought another ABK while C-Note stood against the wall getting choked as the last ABK dug into his pants, trying to find the dope.

A siren sounded and a loud voice came over the P.A. system. *"All inmates get on the ground, now! Stop fighting!"*

Most of the inmates in the yard followed the orders, except for the ones who were fighting. TK and the ABK with the shank had stabbed each other and were still swinging their weapons. They knew whoever put the knife down first would die. B-Dog and another ABK were rolling on the ground, still fighting, and Buck Wild and Pop Somethin' were still going toe-to-toe until Pop landed a haymaker that dropped him. The ABK who was choking C-Note rushed Pop Somethin'. A hard right cross broke the ABK's nose, knocking him out.

A loud pop sounded as smoking canisters landed in their midst. White gas shot out, filling the air. As soon as the gas was inhaled, the choking began. In a few seconds the fight was over and everybody was on the ground. The guards rushed the yard wearing gas masks and riot gear.

***

"Crabtree! Nurse wants to see you," a guard called, banging on the cell door.

Pop Somethin' sat the book down and rolled over. "We got rec in twenty minutes. Fuck that nurse shit, I wanna go outside."

"You can still go to rec. Nurse wants to see you for a quick check-up. C'mon. Cuff up."

Pop Somethin' slipped on the state-issued, soft-bottomed orange shoes and orange top before walking to the door. A slot opened and he stuck his hands out. After cuffs were put on his wrists, the cell door opened and the guards locked him in a waist restraint.

"Jeez, man. What the hell do you eat?" the CO commented, intimidated by Pop Somethin's size.

"Everything. Y'all need to double up them trays, 'cause I'm losin' weight in this bitch-ass hole."

"Yeah, well, this is typically what happens when you break two guys' faces.

"C'mon, Winters. You know I'm a humble man."

"Right. And I'm the Pope."

The exam room was next to the officers' station. Pop Somethin' seemed to fill the small room when he walked in. A smile spread across his face when he saw Ms. Raccara. She was the finest woman who worked in the prison. Everybody with a Y chromosome was checking for the Columbian beauty. The tight-fitting pink scrubs showed off her banging body.

"Glad you could make it today, Mr. Crabtree. Are you behaving yourself?"

Pop Somethin' held her dark brown gaze as he was helped onto the nurse's table. "C'mon, Ms. Raccara, you know I don't cause no trouble."

"Sit back and relax. If you don't cause trouble, why are you in segregation?"

"I had a disagreement."

"Why is it every time you have a disagreement, guys get their bones broken and stabbed?"

"I plead the fifth."

"I bet. So, I called you in to check your bruises and get your vitals. Do you have any pain?"

"Yeah. You makin' my heart hurt."

The nurse blushed as she took his blood pressure. "Besides your heart, are you okay?"

"I am now."

She turned red, shaking her head. "You have this big beard, so I can't tell if your bruises have healed. I need to touch your face. Tell me if this hurts."

When the nurse stepped between his legs, their bodies touched. The guards stood at the door, watching her examine him. Since they were behind the nurse, they couldn't see Pop Somethin's hands squeezing her breasts.

"Does this hurt?"

"Nah. It feels good."

She pressed his cheekbones. "What about this?"

"Nah. I'm good."

The nurse forced herself to step away from him, her face and body flushed from the excitement and danger. Pop Somethin's lap showed how excited he was. "Everything looks fine. You need to stay out of the hole and out of trouble."

"Shit, I'll do you one better. I get out in six months. Then we won't have to worry 'bout the hole or C.O.'s watchin'. I'ma be at chu fo' sho."

The smile on her face and in her eyes told him what her lips couldn't say. She was feeling him. She wanted to fuck. The only reason they hadn't was because she needed her job and didn't want to risk getting caught, but she always let him get his feel on. Always.

***

"Good lookin' on savin' my ass, bruh. I don't know why you did it, but good lookin'," C-Note said, staring out of the cage he was in. He was at segregation rec. Twice a week everyone in the hole got the opportunity to spend an hour outside in a small dog cage. Pop Somethin' was in a cage across from him, doing push-ups.

"That wasn't about you, C-Note. I don't stand up for niggas that don't stand up for theyself. Me and Buck got history. Them niggas tried that same shit to me when I first got here. I fought back, and them niggas fucked me up. When I got my weight up, I brought pain on them niggas. Been on ever since."

"I still appreciate what you did. Them niggas savages. I don't stand a chance against them. I'm five-foot-seven and 160 pounds. I go home in three weeks. I don't wanna go home wit' my shit fucked up."

"If a nigga don't stand up, niggas gon' stand on 'im."

"Yeah, I hear you, bruh, but I ain't cut out for this prison war shit. I get money, fuck bitches, and fire iron."

Pop laughed. "They took the guns at the front door."

"I know. That's why I ain't neva comin' back to this shit. I spent my two years in them books. I'm finna go home and do it big. Turn that dirty money clean and live like them rich white boys. I heard you gettin' out soon. I got a spot on my team. You did me a favor, so I owe you one. Favor for a favor."

Pop Somethin' eyed C-Note, sizing him up. "Fuck you talkin' 'bout, nigga?"

"Niggas say you was a legend in Houston. Had the whole city shook. I wanna nigga like you on my team. I'm from Dallas. I get money, bruh. When you get out, fuck wit' me."

"You gon' offer a nigga you don't know a slot?"

"Like I say, favor for a favor."

Pop Somethin' blew him off. "Whatever, nigga."

"I'm serious, fam. Tell you what, when I get out, I'ma prove it. I get out in three weeks. Gimme yo' info and I'ma get at chu."

Chapter 2

"Broke niggas to the left! Rich niggas to the right!" C-Note called as he and his niggas walked in the strip club. It was his second day out, and for the second day in a row he was partying.

"We gotta find that bitch from last night. What that ho name was?" Artie asked as the small clique walked in the club like they owned it.

"Skittlez, my nigga. Skittlez," Lucci answered.

"Grab us a table. I'ma hit up the bar," C-Note said, eyeing the bartender. "Lemme get three bottles of Moet."

The curly-haired cutie looked him over from head to toe. C-Note was dressed fresh in Ferragamo. "Stop playin', shawty. I got bandz!" he bragged, slapping three crisp hundred-dollar bills on the bar.

After grabbing the bottles, he went to find his team. They were at a booth surrounded by strippers. "Hold on! I the one that just got out! Bring that ass over here!"

C-Note partied, threw money, and drank Moet like it was water. The stripper on his lap was grinding her ass on his tool as he felt up her body. Skittlez was bad. Long hair, yellow skin, tall, and thick. And she was tatted up.

"So, you comin' to the telly wit' me later, or what?" he asked.

"You cute, but I'm chasin' a check, not a date."

"You can do both at the same time."

She spun to face him. "I ain't one of these thoty-ass bitches that fuck for twenty dollas. You gotta pay to play."

"Stop playin'. I'm C-Note. Every time you say my name, you talkin' money."

She laughed, liking the line. "Okay. Me and my bitch M-n-M get off at two. Meet us in the parking lot. What chu in?"

"Black F-150 on sixes."

She frowned. "Nothin' foreign?"

C-Note felt some type of way about her comment, but didn't let it show. "Not yet. Only been out two days. Stay tuned."

A group entering the club broke up their conversation. The niggas wore ice that shined in the dark. The strippers who danced for C-Note and his boys started easing away.

"Who the fuck is that?"

"You don't know who that is?" Skittlez asked as she stood.

C-Note looked confused. "Nah."

"That's ABLE Team. They movin' and shakin' all over D-Town. And they got money. Sorry, boo-boo."

"Hold on. I thought you was leavin' wit' me?"

"You drive a truck. They got Benzes and Bentleys. I chase a check, not a date."

"Weak-ass bitch."

Skittlez turned to smirk at him, patting her big-ass booty as she walked away.

"Who the fuck is them niggas?" C-Note asked, watching jealously as the strippers flocked to ABLE Team.

"That's Franco an' 'em. Niggas gettin' money now," Lucci said.

"You talkin' 'bout li'l bitch-ass Franco? The nigga Radar used to rob and beat?"

"Yeah. His baby mama got, like, five hunnit thou from some lottery shit, like, a year ago. Niggas ain't looked back. And that's Radar in all-black. He one of they shooters now."

C-Note sipped his bottle and sulked. ABLE Team partied and threw money like it was confetti. "You think he'd fuck wit' me?"

"Nah. Them niggas is day-ones and family. Circle tight."

"But we need a real plug. I thought you niggas was out here eatin' while I was locked up. Fuck you niggas was doin'?"

"We was out here livin', nigga. We got money. You trippin'," Lucci said.

"This ain't no money, bruh. You niggas got a few pounds of weed and a couple bands. Ain't even got lawyer money. Takin' penitentiary chances for a few racks ain't gon' get it. My nigga, it's white boys in the feds for money launderin' and insider tradin'. Seein' millions! They get five years for twenty mill! We out here gettin' fifty years for twenty pounds of loud. That ain't money, my nigga. We just in the way and fillin' up cells."

"Well, I don't know nothin' 'bout pill schemes and tradin' inside. All I know how to do is trap," Artie said.

"I see you was in them books, huh?" Lucci asked.

"Hell yeah, I wanna see some real paper. T just did two years for dope. That shit was hell. I can't go back for chasin' a couple thousand."

"But you coulda got slammed, nigga. They caught you on the highway. Two years state was love."

"That ain't the point. What matter is gettin' it like them white boys."

"So what you wanna do?" Lucci asked. "You the one that read all the books an' shit. How we gon' see real money?"

"I think we should start throwin' club parties."

Lucci and Artie burst out laughing.

"Fuck you niggas laughin' at?"

"You, nigga! Talkin' 'bout throwin' parties. Fuck you gon' make money off that?" Artie laughed.

"That's why you niggas gon' always be workers. Niggas is stupid. Listen. This how we do it. We pay a rapper or singer who kinda washed up to do a show at a club. Charge 75 at the door, 150 for VIP. Clubs can fit a couple hunnit people. We talkin' forty or fifty Gs in one night. Not to mention what we make off the bar and you niggas movin' product. We sow up everything. Liquor, weed, and pills. We do that 'til we get our money up and start buyin' tons of weed and dope. We in Texas, so everythang cheap. Take that shit up north and double our money. Invest in our own clubs and parties to clean our money."

Artie and Lucci wore surprised looks. "Damn, nigga. Yo' ass really was in there gettin' smart an' shit," Artie said.

"What it take to get started?" Lucci asked.

"About twenty or twenty-five racks."

"I got five," Artie said.

"I got three," Lucci said.

C-Note looked disappointed. "That's it?"

"Yeah, nigga," Lucci spoke up. "We got you right, and we been spendin' money for two days."

C-Note was quiet. The wheels churned in his mind as he watched ABLE Team. "Lemme get five hunnit dollas."

"My nigga, we just gave you twenty-five hunnit yesterday," Artie said.

"I went shoppin' and spent my last on them bottles. Just gimme the money, nigga. Trust me."

Artie reluctantly gave him the money. C-Note went to the bar and bought another bottle of Moet before going over to ABLE Team. They were in the champagne room. A bodyguard who looked like D-Bo stopped him at the door.

"What up, li'l man?"

"I wanna holla at Franco."

"Nah. You ain't wit' the team."

"C'mon, bruh. That's my nigga from way back. I just bought him a bottle."

The bodyguard looked him over. "Wait right here." He walked in the VIP room and said a couple words to Franco. Franco looked towards C-Note and nodded. The bodyguard waved him in.

"What's good, C-Note? I see you back out here," Franco smiled as they hugged.

"Yeah. I got out yesterday. Here you go. I bought chu a bottle, my nigga."

Franco smirked at the bottle of Moet. "That's so 2017, my nigga. Only champagne I drink is Aces. I use Moet to gargle after I brush my teeth. Give that shit to one of them hos."

The insult burned, but C-Note didn't let it show. "Yeah, sho'. You know a nigga just touched down, so I'm a li'l behind. Tryin'a catch up."

"Yeah. I know what dat's like. Er'body can't start at the top. Need niggas on the bottom to keep niggas like me on top. Feel me?"

C-Note took the jab on the chin. Franco was clowning him. What made it worse was Franco was a bitch. Radar used to torture him, and now he was his shooter. That was a real bitch move. But C-Note needed a favor, and if being embarrassed would get him what he needed, so be it.

"Yeah, I hear you. But check it out, I wanna talk to you about this business plan. I wanna hire some entertainers to throw parties. Shit real lucrative. I need a partner. What up?"

Franco laughed. "Ludacris? What the fuck you just say?"

"Nah, lucrative. It means you can make money."

"Oh. Okay. I see you was in them books, huh? Check it out, I got my own plans. Me and the team finna hit up New York and talk to some crackers about investin' in a NBA team. I know we go back to them high school days, but ain't no room on the team for new niggas. ABLE Team all about day-ones."

Franco's words crushed C-Note's soul and spirit. Not only did he get rejected, but also humiliated. He left the champagne room with his head down, pride wounded.

"Damn, nigga. You look like he took yo' bitch," Lucci joked.

"Not now, bruh. Let's hit it. I need to figure out how to put us on."

***

"What's wrong, baby?" Star asked, plopping down on the couch. C-Note took his eyes off the basketball game and looked at her. She was the only female who stood by him during his bid, visiting faithfully every week. She brought seven grams of loud every trip. If it wasn't for her, he would've starved.

And as much as he appreciated her for holding him down, he wasn't feeling her. She wanted a man, and he wasn't trying to be that. Plus she had three kids and three baby daddies. On top of that, she was chubby and a rock toss away from tying ugly. She looked like Serena Williams without makeup. The only reason he noticed her was her big lips, big titties, and big booty, but the big gut fucked her body up and gave her a 'booty do' – a term for when her stomach sticks out more than her booty do.

"I'm just thinkin' 'bout how to get this paper. Shit ain't workin' out how I planned."

"You gotta give it some time, baby. You just got out. You always said the Great Wall of China wasn't built overnight. I believe in you. You the smartest nigga I ever met. Just give it some time. You figure it out."

Her words brought a smile to his face. "Damn, gurl. You cold wit' them words, you know that?"

"Yeah, Daddy, I'm cold wit' my mouth, too. Wanna see?" She was unzipping his pants before he could respond. After she freed his dick, she deep-throated him, her big lips feeling like a vacuum as she sucked him. She massaged his balls, even taking them in her mouth and humming. When he busted his nut. She swallowed it all, and when his dick went limp, she sucked him back hard.

"Now come in the room and fuck me in all my holes. I told you I'ma be yo' porn star."

In the bedroom there was no romancing or foreplay. They got naked and C-Note pinned her knees to her chest and fucked her, drilling her pussy. Her stomach and titties jiggled in unison as she called his name. When he got tired of her ugly fuck-faces, he flipped her over. After sliding on a condom, he got behind her and fucked her in the ass. Star loved it, fingering her pussy as he pounded her asshole. He came hard.

When C-Note was about to bust, he snatched off the rubber and started jagging off.

"Come get it, bitch."

Star spun around and started sucking his dick again, tugging at his balls. When he busted again, she swallowed every drop.

Chapter 3

The phone vibrating on the table woke C-Note from his sleep. He checked the screen. It was a call from someone in prison. He pressed one. "Yeah?"

"C-Note, what's good, nigga?"

"What up, Pop Somethin'? I was wonderin' when you was gon' call, nigga."

"I was trynna let you settle in. Niggas be movin' fast when they first get out. Plus I'm still in the hole. You know we can't use the phones every day in the box."

"Damn, I forgot about that. Did you get them flicks and money receipt?"

"Yeah. Good lookin', bruh. That five hunnit was right on time. I thought you was anotha one of them jackin'-ass niggas, but chu showin' and provin'."

"I don't do no jackin', bruh. My word is solid."

"That's one hunnit. Who these hos in these flicks? I need a bitch."

"Just some thots on Facebook and Instagram. Bitches flexin' for likes."

"Well, like them hos for me. Damn, they bad. I can't stop jaggin' off."

"C'mon, bruh! I don't need to know all that," C-Note laughed

"I'm just keepin' that shit real. But on some other shit, I need you to do me a favor. I ain't heard from my li'l cousin, Shanice, in a minute. Can you find her for me? I got her old address and phone number. Can you do somethin' with that? See if she need anything and let her know I'm gettin' out in a couple months."

"Don't trip, my nigga. Gimme the info. I'ma have Star look her up. She good on them computers."

After talking to Pop Somethin' for fifteen minutes and getting his cousin's info, C-Note made calls to Lucci and Artie. Tonight was a big night, and he needed his niggas ready.

***

"Man, I don't know about this," Lucci warned.
"Get off that scaredy-ass shit. We need this money. How else we gon' get it?" C-Note asked.
"I feel what Lucci sayin'. I ain't trynna end up in jail for this shit," Artie added.
"You niggas takin' penitentiary chances every day when y'all hustle. We finna get it all in one shot. Quit trippin'."
"Damn, nigga!" Lucci fussed. "If we get shot or go to jail, I'm whoopin' yo' ass!"
"You sure the nigga outta town?" Artie asked.
"Yeah. He in New York. I already got all the info. She come here to work out every other day. We gon make her give us the money."

***

C-Note kept a half a block of distance between the stolen truck he drove and the red Porsche. He had already made the drive twice. When he was sure the car wouldn't detour from the normal path, he sped ahead. They were waiting on the side of the garage when the Porsche pulled in. Before the door was able to close, they were in the garage.
C-Note pointed a gun at the driver. "Don't scream. Get outta the car slow. How many people in the house?"

She moved slowly, letting him see her every move. She was terrified, and her body shook as she spoke. "Just my kids and my sister. If you lookin' for Franco, he out of town. I don't know when he comin' back."

"Take us in the house. Don't scream. We ain't gon' hurt nobody. We just want the money."

"He don't keep no money here."

C-Note knew she was lying. "We will see."

In the house they found the sister in the kitchen, cooking. Three toddlers sat at the table, eating. An infant was asleep in a car seat that sat on the counter.

"We ain't trynna hurt nobody. Give us the safe and we gone."

Franco's wife spoke up. "I just told y'all we don't keep no money in the house. He out of town. We don't know nothin'."

Lucci mugged C-Note, upset he had put them on a bogus mission. C-Note ignored the look. There was money in the house. He knew it. Franco bragged too much and talked too much shit. A nigga like that kept money around. There was a safe in the house. He knew it.

He looked at the baby. The sister grabbed it out of the car seat. "Is that yo' baby?"

She nodded. "Please don't hurt my baby."

"I won't. Just gimme the money. I know it's some money in this house. Let me get it."

The females were scared and on the verge of tears, but Franco's girl stayed true to her words. "I told you we don't have no money."

C-Note pointed the gun at her sister. "Gimme the baby!"

"No! Please. Don't take my baby!"

He snatched the baby from her arms roughly and walked over to the microwave. The baby began to cry loudly. "I'ma cook yo' baby if yo' sister don't tell me where the money at."

"Michelle, tell him! Franco got some more money. They gon' leave. Just give it to them."

Franco's wife hesitated. C-Note put the baby in the microwave and closed the door.

"Okay! Okay!" Michelle shouted. "It's upstairs."

***

"Damn! That shit got me geeked. I feel like I just snorted a eight ball," Lucci laughed.

Artie's eyes were wide with fear. "Man, I was scared as fuck. I ain't neva doin' that shit no more."

"Fuck that shit, nigga. How much money we got?" C-Note asked, looking back and forth from the road to Lucci.

"A li'l bit over fifty racks."

Artie looked amazed. "Damn! Fifty Gs that quick? We might have to do that shit again."

C-Note spoke up. "Ain't no need. We got what we came for. I'ma turn that fifty into one hunnit. This petty hustlin' shit is over. Them Able Team niggas think they seein' money, but we gon' pass them niggas up. Watch."

***

"I found some information on that girl you wanted. She pretty. Who is she?"

C-Note held his finger in the air, signaling Star to hold on. He was taking an important call. "Yeah, I'm at Club

Geek in Dallas. I want him to come to a party I'm throwin'." He paused to listen. "Couple songs. Yeah. Club can fit about five hunnit people. Liquor and a few other amenities is on the house." He listened again. "Thirty days from today. We need time to market. Tell Waka to call me personally. Everything set on my end. Thanks for yo' time."

"How did it go?" Star asked after he hung up.

"Shit lookin' good. I gotta holla at the nigga that own the club again, get the fliers, and holla at Waka, but the foundation is set."

"I knew you could do it," Star exclaimed, leaning forward to kiss him. C-Note turned his head aside, accepting her kiss on the cheek. Star noticed the dis, but didn't say anything. "I gotta take the kids to they doctor appointments. Do you need me to do anything while I'm out?"

"Nah. I'ma be out and about. I got some moves to make."

"Okay. I found that girl on Facebook. Who is she?"

"That's my nigga li'l cousin. He still locked up and wanted me to find her for him. Good lookin' out. What's her info?"

"*Imsoshanice*. She pretty. You sure she yo' friend cousin?"

He looked up from his phone. "Seriously? We finna do this?"

"I'm sorry, baby. I'm feelin' a li'l insecure. You don't talk about us no more. Ever since you got out, you been distant. I'm just wonderin' how you feel about me. About us."

He took a deep breath. "Listen, how about we talk about this later? I got a lotta shit on my plate, and you

need to get the kids to the doctor. But I never lied to you, and I ain't about to start now. I don't know her. She my nigga cousin. He asked me to find her. That's it."
    A grin crept onto her face. "Okay. I believe you. I trust you. See you later."
    When she leaned in for another kiss, C-Note accepted it on the lips. Star's smile got bigger. She gathered the kids and left.
    As soon as the door closed, he looked up Shanice on Facebook. She was beyond fine. Redbone, long hair, slanted eyes, nice lips. After sending her a friend request, he went to shit and shower.
    He had just stepped out of the water when the doorbell rang. He wrapped a towel around his waist and went to answer. It was the neighbor, Deidra. She ogled C-Note's wet body. He was five-foot-seven and 160 pounds, but Deidra looked at him like he was LeBron James.
    "Oh, damn. Did I catch you at a bad time?" she asked.
    "Nah, I was just gettin' out the shower. What up?"
    "I was wondering if you had some more loud. I need a seven."
    "Yeah. Come in." He checked out her body as he locked the door. Deidra was short and petite with some big-ass titties. She didn't have much ass, so her body looked like a capital P. She also knew C-Note didn't sell weed. He figured she was on some freaky shit, and since he had just gotten an ounce from Lucci, he wanted to see how far she would go.
    After going to the room and breaking off some of his stash, he walked back into the living room. "I don't got a scale, but this more than a seven."
    She' dropped the money on the table and took the weed. "Good lookin' out."

"Yeah. I'm 'bout to be throwin' a party at Club Geek next month. Waka doin' a show. Bring some friends and come support yo' boy."

"What? You throwin' parties now?"

"Yeah. I'm trynna get it. Shit gon' be lit. Come show love."

"Fo' sho'. Just let me know when. Me and my girls gon' show up and shut it down," she laughed, shaking her titties.

C-Note stared at her chest. "How big is them muthafuckas?"

She poked her breasts out proudly. "Thirty-four F's."

"Damn! Let me see."

She looked unsure. "You got a girl. You betta stop."

"You know I don't sell weed. And I know you just seen Star leave. We grown. We can do what we want."

When C-Note dropped the towel, Deidra sat the weed on the table and went for his dick. He stopped her. "Get naked. Be right back."

He went to the room and grabbed a bottle of flavored sex oil. Deidra was naked when he walked back into the living room. When he saw her body, his dick got extra hard. She had a caramel complexion and a firm body. Her titties were super big and had dark nipples. Her pussy was shaved, and she had a small gap between her thighs.

He lay her on the couch, oiled up her breasts, and started titty-fucking her. Every time his dick came out of the top of her cleavage, it went right in her mouth. He fucked her chest like it was a pussy, busting a nut all over her chest, chin, and lips.

She used the towel to wipe herself before lying on the couch and spreading her legs. "Now let me get mine," she said, rubbing her pussy.

C-Note got between her legs and gave her what she wanted. He sucked her pearl and fucked her with two fingers. When she came, he flipped her over and fucked her from the back. Her pussy was so good he didn't pull out when he busted.

"Damn, gurl. You got that fiya!"

"Snap back, nigga. You ain't know?"

"Look, I ain't trynna be rude, but I got moves to make. But I definitely wanna get up wit' chu again."

"I know how it is. I ain't trippin'. Just hit a bitch up every now and then. I like you and wanna fuck wit' chu. Star can have Tuesdays and Thursdays. I'ma keep you satisfied on the weekend."

After getting dressed, C-Note left the house to meet up with Gena, the owner of Club Geek. They finalized the contract and C-Note gave him five thousand dollars before leaving.

He checked his phone as he climbed into the truck. Shanice had accepted his friend request. A flash of excitement passed through him as he sent her a message.

i'm c-note. pop said get at u. w/u?

u know my cuz?

i was locked up w/him.

wat up?

pop wanna know if u gud?

yeah.

he want number.

When the number popped up on his screen, he called her.

"Hello?"

"Ay, Shanice. This C-Note. What up?"

"Hey. Where my cousin?"

A GANGSTER'S CODE

"Still locked up, but he gettin' out in a couple months. He wanted me to get at you and see if you needed anything."

"Oh. Um, I'm good. When you talk to him, tell him I'm sorry for not writing in a while. Shit been crazy. But I will."

"If you want I can add yo' line to my account so he can call you."

"That would be cool. I miss my nigga. Thank you."

"It ain't shit. Can I meet you somewhere? I got a li'l paper he wanted me to give you."

"Yeah. Can you come to my house? I live in Fort Worth. I get off work at six."

"I ain't that far. I'm in Dallas. What's the address?"

***

After parking the truck, C-Note sent the text. The front door of a red and blue house opened a couple moments later. Shanice walked out carrying a baby girl on her hip. She looked better in person. Long, thick black hair, glowing reddish-brown skin, and the blue business skirt and heels showed off a body that would cause car accidents.

C-Note strolled up to the porch with extra sauce in his walk. "What up, Shanice? I know you prolly hear this a lot, but damn, you fine."

She blushed, adjusting the baby on her hip. "Thanks. You know my cousin probably wouldn't like you flirting with me."

"I'm not flirtin'. I'm bein' real. Plus, Pop ain't here. Just me and you."

33

Shanice looked away uncomfortably. He noticed the change in her demeanor and chilled with the compliments. "I got a couple hunnit for you. If you need anything, just holla. Pop Somethin' saved my ass while I was in, and I owe the nigga. Lookin' out for you ain't shit compared to what that nigga did for me."

"Thanks so much. You called just in time. The daycare bills is kickin' my ass."

"How many kids you got?"

"Just her, but it's hard when you doin' it by yourself."

"So you don't got no man? Where her daddy at?"

Shanice looked away. "It's a long story."

"I'm down to listen. You got my number. Hit me up."

She smiled. "You, don't want my problems. Trust me."

"We all got problems. If you ever wanna escape, I'm throwin' a party next month at Club Geek. Waka performin'. You can be my special guest."

"Thanks, but no thanks. I don't –" A look of terror flashed in her eyes. "Uh, you gotta leave. Tell Pop to call me."

C-Note turned to see what had caused her reaction. A blue suburban was parking behind his F-150. A big, black nigga got out, mean-mugging. C-Note felt like he was being approached by the ABKs again. This nigga was huge, over six feet tall, muscles bulging like he just got out of jail. When he walked onto the porch, C-Note could smell liquor coming from his pores.

"Fuck you doin' at my house, nigga?"

"It ain't like that, bruh. I just came –"

"Get the fuck off my porch, nigga! I don't wanna hear that bitch-ass shit!"

Shanice stepped between the men. "Nitty, don't do this. He Pop Somethin's friend. He just came through with some money from Pop."

"Don't you see men's havin' a conversation, bitch? Don't say shit when men is talkin'!"

C-Note took a couple steps back, hand close to his waist. "I ain't trynna cause no problems, bruh. I just came to drop off this money."

"Fuck you still doin' on my porch, nigga? Fuck outta here!" Nitty barked, making a move toward C-Note. He stopped when the .357 Magnum pointed at his chest.

"Hold on, nigga! You doin' too much," C-Note said, cocking the hammer as he stepped off the porch.

"Yeah, li'l nigga. You betta have heat. Next time I see you, I'ma have mine."

"Only reason it's gon' be a next time cause yo' wifey and daughter right here. When you see me in the streets, get at me."

A GANGSTER'S CODE

Chapter 4

"Pop Somethin', what's good?"

"Damn, nigga, you turnt! Screamin' all in my ear an' shit. Yo' background loud as fuck."

"The party gettin' started. This bitch is lit! Wish you was here, my nigga."

"I'll be out there soon. Aye, I need you to go somewhere a li'l quiet. I need to holla at chu."

"A'ight. I'm walkin' toward the back office now. What's good?"

"Good lookin' on gettin' at Shanice for me. She told me you been lookin' out for her."

"That ain't shit, my nigga. I told you I got chu. That's what you wanted to holla about?"

"Nah, I wanna know about her nigga, Nitty. What up wit' that nigga?"

C-Note paused. The last time he'd seen Nitty wasn't good. Pop Somethin' had enough stress being locked up, and he didn't want to add to it by telling him Shanice was letting a nigga put his hands on her. "What you mean?"

"Somethin' wrong. Every time the nigga come around, she act like she can't talk and get off the phone. She won't tell me nothin' 'bout him. Who is he? What he be on?"

"I only seen the nigga once, and I don't know shit about him. He seem like a typical nigga. Shanice is bad, so the nigga got in his fag body about me be in by the spot."

"You checked that nigga, right?"

"I upped my dog and told that nigga to be cool before I got up outta there."

"On everything I love, if this bitch-ass nigga treatin' my li'l cousin –"

"Don't even sweat that shit, Pop. Shanice a big girl. She can handle herself. She ain't the li'l girl she was when you left. She a mother. A grown woman. She good."

"A'ight. You right. G'on back to the party. And make sure you send me some pictures, nigga!"

***

The club was packed. Everybody was vibing, drinking, and having a good time. As Lucci and Artie moved around hustling, C-Note counted the profits in his mind. At least sixty thousand, and fifty was his.

Deidra's big-ass bouncing titties made him forget about the money and come back to the party. She was wearing a tight, black dress that had her titties spilling out the top. "What up, shawty? I see you made it. You sure yo' girls gon' be able to stay in the house?" he asked, ogling her breasts.

"I told you me and my bitches was comin'. And I wore this so you could have easy access to 'em. I know you comin' to kick it wit' me later, right?"

"I gotta find somethin' to do wit' Star. She stalkin' me all over the club."

"I told you to leave that ugly bitch. Them ain't cho kids."

"It ain't that easy. Loyalty to a nigga locked up gotta be rewarded."

"Well, stay wit' her ugly ass, then. I just wanna know if I can get some pipe tonight."

A GANGSTER'S CODE

"I'ma see what I can do. I need to get back in that juice box. Let me go check on somethin'. I'ma send you a bottle."

"Hey! That's what I'm talkin' 'bout!" Deidra sang, giving him a hug before sashaying away.

"Why you huggin' her?"

C-Note spun around and seen Star mugging him. "C'mon, Star. We ain't finna do this," he said before walking away.

"C-Note! C-Note!" she screamed after him. "I know you hear me callin' you!"

Partygoers began whispering as they looked at Star and C-Note. He ignored everybody and headed to the VIP section. Security stopped him on the way.

"Somebody outside say they know you. I don't see 'em on the list."

"Who is it?"

"Two females."

"They bad?"

The big man smiled lustfully. "Bad and boujee."

"Let's go check it out."

When C-Note stepped outside, his eyes almost popped out of his head. Every time he'd seen Shanice, she looked better. Her hair was whipped in long Beyoncé curls, and the powder-blue dress she wore had niggas and females watchin' her every move. And the female that stood next to her was just as hot.

"Damn, baby! You shuttin' shit down! Why you ain't call and let me know you was comin'?"

"Honestly, I didn't want to bother you. I came at the last minute because my cousin wanted to see Waka."

"I'm glad you came. C'mon. Follow me. I got a spot for y'all in VIP."

The party and concert was a hit. Waka did his thang and was in the crowd, mingling with party-goers. C-Note did the same thing, letting everybody know he would be throwing parties once a month for a year. He had just left a table of women, heading to the VIP section to check on Shanice.

"What's goin' on in this section? Y'all enjoyin' the party?"

"Hell yeah! We turnt!" Shanice said, walking over and hugging him. "Thanks for lettin' us in. Waka did it. I needed to let my hair down."

"Glad to hear it. I wish you woulda told me you was comin' so I coulda made a li'l time to kick it wit' chu."

"Nah, don't trip. I know you gotta work. We havin' a ball. This was a last minute decision to come. I finally got a little free time and I'm happy I let Meghan talk me into comin'."

"So, where Nitty at? He don't look like the kinda nigga that would let you outta his sight. Especially not to come to a club."

Shanice let out a deep sigh, rolling her eyes. "I don't even want to think about my baby daddy. Not tonight. I just want to –"

"So, this how you gon' do me? Just flirt wit' bitches in my face all night like I ain't standin' here?" C-Note spun around and saw Star storming toward him, her face twisted in a mug, eyes wide with anger.

"What is you on, shawty? Chill."

"Nah! Fuck that! You put these pretty bitches in VIP. Don't think I don't know what that is."

C-Note raised his voice. "Aye. You need to chill wit' that jealous-ass shit! That's my nigga cousin. G'on wit' this insecure shit. I'm tryna work and get money."

"You the one that made me insecure. You don't fuck me no more, and you always turn yo' face when I try to kiss you. When you was locked up, you used to stick yo' tongue down my throat and talk about how you was gon' fuck me. Now that you out, you wanna change up."

"Look, we ain't finna do this right now. Go home. I'ma holla at chu later."

"Go home? Fuck you, nigga! You ain't my daddy. I stood by yo' ass when you was locked up, and this how you do me? I bet Shanice won't bring yo' ass no weed."

"We ain't finna do this. I ain't goin' there wit' chu. Security! Get her outta here!"

When Star realized what was about to happen, she snapped. She pushed C-Note, making him stumble and fall on his ass. Then she rushed Shanice, swinging her arms like a windmill, her long and sharp nails aiming for the pretty woman's face.

Shanice recognized Star was trying to scratch her face up. She knew ugly women hated her on sight, and she was ready. When Star ran at her, swinging wildly, Shanice side-stepped and grabbed her sew-in weave, yanking hard. When Star lost her balance, Shanice drilled her with lefts and rights.

Security jumped in, grabbing Shanice in a bear hug. Star shook off her dizziness, noticing the guards had Shanice hemmed up, she figured this was her opportunity to get her licks back. She rushed Shanice, ready to do damage, but movement out the corner of her eye made her flinch. Meghan was swinging a Moet bottle at her head.

Star fell to the floor, limp as if all the bones had been snatched from her body.

***

"I hope you done with that crazy-ass girl," Shanice laughed.

C-Note took his eyes off the road and looked at his passenger. "I don't know what I was thinkin' 'bout fuckin' wit' her. She came through when a nigga was in a jam and I felt I owed her."

"I hear you. But damn, she was crazy."

"Talkin' 'bout crazy, where you get them hands from? I didn't know you could get down like that."

"Bitches hated on me all my life. They think 'cause I'm pretty I ain't 'bout that action. Pop made sure I knew how to handle myself."

"Damn. My nigga woulda been proud. And you know we got that crazy shit in common, right? 'Cause Nitty crazy as fuck! How you start fuckin' wit' a nigga like that?"

"I don't know. Young and stupid. Paul – I mean Pop Somethin' – didn't want me fuckin' niggas in the hood. Shit, he didn't even want me to have a boyfriend. I rebelled. Plus, Nitty kinda reminded me of my cousin. Niggas in Fort Worth was scared of Nitty like niggas in Houston was scared of Pop. It was exciting at first. Then, once I got pregnant, shit got real. I want to raise my daughter with a mother and father, so I put up wit' a lot o' bullshit. He don't work or help support us. It's really on me. All he do is drink, smoke, and blow powder. Every now and then he'll bring some money home from a hustle. But I still love his no-good ass."

"Pop asked me about him the other day. I didn't know what to say. Why you won't tell him 'bout Nitty?"

"Pop Somethin' is crazy. He would kill Nitty if he knew all the shit he put me through. I don't want him to kill my daughter's father, so I don't tell him about Nitty."

"Shit. Pop finna get out. What you gon' do then?"

Shanice breathed deep, staring out at the dark road. "I don't know. I'll cross that bridge when I get to it, but I don't wanna talk about my baby daddy no more. He got his third DUI and gotta spend the weekend in jail. I just want to relax and chill."

"I hear you. What you wanna do? Meghan found her some company and the night is still young"

Shanice gave him a sexy smile, mischief shining in her eyes. "You the man with the master plan. You lead."

It only took ten minutes to get to the hotel. Lips started smacking as soon as the door closed. Clothes flew all over the floor. When Shanice was naked, C-Note laid her on the bed and checked out her body. Her long, black hair pooled around her face, neck, and shoulders like a shiny mink coat. Seductive, almond-shaped dark eyes watched him. Luscious lips looked like they were ready to scream his name. She had full C-cup breasts and big, brown nipples, a flat stomach, and toned thighs. Her pussy was bald. C-Note could feel pre-cum drip from the tip of his dick as he watched her. When he couldn't take it no more, he moved to the bed and snatched her legs open.

"Oh, shit!" Shanice moaned, grabbing the back of his head as he sucked her clit. When her orgasm began building, she bucked her hips and smashed his face against her pussy, and then she came. It was loud. "Oh, shit! Oh, shit, C-Note! Oh, shit!"

When her body stopped shivering, C-Note smiled, wiping the cum off his mouth. "Damn, girl. You taste like candy."

Shanice sat up and began sucking and kissing her juices off his lips. "You right. I do taste like candy. Now put that rubber on and let's make the neighbors know yo' name."

After putting on the protection, C-Note slid between her legs and into her promised land. Every time he pushed inside of her, Shanice threw it back at him, matching his strokes. His first nut came quickly. After changing rubbers, he flipped Shanice over and hit it from the back. Her ass bounced and jiggled like crazy as he fucked her. Shanice continued matching his stroke. Every time he thrust forward, she threw her ass back at him. He slapped her yellow ass cheeks, leaving red handprints across her booty. Shanice loved it, growling and moaning.

C-Note could feel his second nut coming on. He prolonged it for as long as he could. His body got stiff as he filled the rubber. In the back of his mind, he knew he had to have Shanice. He didn't care what Nitty or Pop Somethin' had to say.

A GANGSTER'S CODE

Chapter 5

"Pop Somethin'! What it do, nigga? Welcome home!" Smoke grinned, opening his arms for an aggressive bear hug.

"Smoke! What up, nigga? Look at chu, boy. You fat as fuck!" Pop Somethin' grinned.

"We don't work out and lift weights in the real world. Plus, I ain't neva met a nigga big enough to stand in the way of some hot shit."

"Chuch!" Pop agreed.

"Look at chu, nigga. Damn! What, you on some Incredible Hulk shit? You know that extra-large t-shirt is way too small," Smoke cracked.

Pop Somethin' had stuffed his six-foot-six, 240-pound frame into a 2X black Robin t-shirt, Robin jeans, and black retro Jordans. "This a 2X, nigga. And where my food at?" Pop asked, looking through the windows of the 2010 Magnum.

"That's what you worried about, nigga? You ain't had no pussy in eight years, and you worried about some food? Yo' priorities sound fucked up."

Pop ignored the dig and opened the car door. There was a bag on the backseat. "I know it betta be some food in this bag or we fightin'."

"Didn't I just tell yo' muscle-bound ass I don't fight?"

Pop didn't answer. There was food in the bag, and he climbed in the backseat to bust it down. BBQ ribs, macaroni and cheese, fluffy buttermilk biscuits, coleslaw, and apple pie.

Smoke laughed when he seen how Pop reacted to the food. "You know when it's two people in a car, you s'posed to take the passenger seat."

"Quit it wit' the jokes, nigga. You got what I holla'ed at you 'bout?" Pop asked in between bites of the food.

Smoke reached into the glove box and handed Pop a brown paper bag. "I see you still serious as fuck and don't know how to laugh."

"Niggas get killed for playin' too much."

"Yeah, you still the same nigga. Just bigger. So, what you wanna do? Hit the hood? The mall? Find some hos? See the fam?"

"Nah. Lemme see yo' phone. I need to get up wit' Deso. I told that nigga I was gon' holla at him my first day out."

"Deso stay in the hood. Hoodrat-ass nigga. All he do is bleed the block."

After making a phone call, Pop Somethin' directed Smoke to an abandoned parking lot. A silver Infinity truck was already parked there. Pop checked the contents of the paper bag as Smoke parked next to the truck. A pistol, lighter, and small bottle of gasoline were inside.

"Ain't nobody in that truck. Deso lost his shit," Smoke said, looking around the lot for signs life.

"Put the car in park and put cho hands on the steering wheel," Pop ordered,

Smoke looked in the rearview mirror and seen the Glock 40 pointed at his head. "Pop, what the fuck you doin', nigga? Put that muthafuckin' gun down!"

"I ain't gon' tell you no more. Park the car and put cho hands on the steering wheel."

Smoke did as he was told. "This fucked up, bruh. I been knowin' you since we was in grade school. This how you do me? Fuck is this shit about?"

"You got some money, nigga?"

"You know I do. I s'posed to take you shoppin'. That's what this about? Some money?"

"Nah, nigga. It's about loyalty."

Smoke looked confused. "Fuck you talkin' 'bout, nigga?"

"Clutch and Scrap."

Surprise showed on Smoke's face. "I don't got shit to do wit' them niggas."

"Them niggas tried to off me. I heard you told them niggas where my people stay so they could get the jump on me and get me out the way. Niggas popped me up, and I went to the pen for baggin' Clutch. It's yo' fault."

"That's some bullshit, Pop! You know you my nigga. I wouldn't do that. Who told you some shit like that?"

"Deso. And a couple niggas I was locked down wit'. Deso wanted to off yo' ass a long time ago, but I told him not to touch you. Only reason I ain't pushed yo' shit back yet is 'cause I wanna know why you set me up. If you lie, I'm killin' yo' whole family. I love yo' moms like she birthed me, but if you lie, I'ma put a bullet in her face."

Smoke hung his head. His life was over. He didn't bother pleading for forgiveness. It was no use. He had crossed the devil and failed. The only thing he could do was save his family. "Clutch and Scrap said you hit 'em for some birdies and fifty sacks. They gave me a brick to tell 'em where yo' aunty stay. At the time I was fucked up and needed the money."

Pop stared in Smoke's eyes through the rearview mirror. He seen the truth and fear. Everybody was scared to die. "You know the love of money is the root of all evil? I almost got knocked off, and them crackers took eight years of my life for baggin' Clutch. All because you wanted some money."

Smoke mugged Pop Somethin'. "Fuck a sermon, nigga. Do what you gotta do."

Pop!

Blood, brain, and skull fragments splattered the windshield. Smoke slumped in the seat, dead. Pop Somethin' closed his eyes and took a big sniff. The smell of fresh blood and gun powder filled his nostrils. He smiled. The beast was out of the cage.

He searched Smoke and found five Gs in his pocket. After taking the money, he poured gasoline all over the car's interior, then took a few steps back and tossed a lit match toward the car. Pop retreated a safe distance away, then stood and watched the car until it was fully engulfed in flames. When he was satisfied all evidence of him being in the car was gone, he hopped in the Infinity.

***

Pop checked the piece of paper one more time. The address matched what was written in the letter. The house looked like a mini-mansion: manicured grass, trimmed bushes, nice paint job. This wasn't what he was used to, and he felt uncomfortable in the upper-class neighborhood.

After tucking the .40 Glock in his waist, he got out of the truck and walked up to the house. The doorbell sounded like a song playing on a church piano.

A couple of seconds later, somebody spoke behind the door. "Who dat?"

"Pop Somethin'."

When the door opened, a tall, skinny nigga appeared. He had dark skin, a nappy fro, and a chip on his front tooth. "Look at dis nigga! Damn, Pop! You got big as fuck!"

"Deso! What's good, boy?" The men hugged like they were long-lost brothers, Pop Somethin' swallowing the smaller man up in his arms as they embraced.

"You got them dreads and beard like them Muslim niggas. Don't tell me you went in and got all religious an' shit."

"Stop playin', nigga. You know I'm 'bout that Rasta life!"

"Fo' sho, my nigga. C'mon in. Come meet the squad."

"Look like you doin' good, nigga. How the fuck you get this house?"

"My bitch got this from her granny when she died." Then Deso stopped and got serious. "Where that fag-ass nigga Smoke?"

"You know I don't play. That nigga in the parkin' lot."

Deso nodded and smiled before leading Pop Somethin' through the foyer. The inside of the house was a lot different from the outside. Liquor bottles, clothes, and old food containers were strewn over the living room. Lounged around on couches were three grimy-looking niggas who looked ready to take anything with value.

Deso introduced everybody. "This Pop Squad. Drama. Yae. Snot. Y'all, this my nigga, Pop Somethin'."

Pop nodded at everybody.

"We know who you is," a light-skinned nigga with nappy dreads spoke up. "I'm Yae. You a legend in H-Town. I love meetin' real niggas. Too many pussy-niggas out here in da way."

"Dat's why we fuck dem pussy boys!" Drama laughed, showing a row of gold teeth.

Snot pulled a bag of lime-green weed from his pocket. "You smoke?"

Pop reached for the bag. "Hell yeah!"

"You can have dat. Shit was free. Fucked a pussy-nigga over for a couple pounds of dat shit." Snot laughed, tossing Pop Somethin' blunt wrap.

"You got some pussy yet, nigga?" Deso asked.

"Nah. I only been out for 'bout an hour."

"We got some stripper bitches in the back. Dey wit' da team, and dey know how to treat a real nigga," Drama said.

Pop gave Deso a look. "What he talkin' 'bout?"

"They my bitch-bitches. They valid."

"And they fuckin'? Just like that?"

"They wit' the team, my nigga. Follow me."

The house had four bedrooms and two and a half bathrooms. It also had a pool out back and a den in the basement. Pop Somethin' puffed the blunt as he followed Deso into a bedroom at the back of the house. Two females slept in a bed. "Dis Princess and Queenie. They twins," Deso explained before slapping one of them on the ass. Pop could see her flesh jiggle under the sheet.

"Aye! What the fuck!" she snapped. Angry eyes opened, mean-mugging Pop and Deso. "Damn, nigga! What the fuck you doin'?"

Even though she had sleep in her eyes from just waking up, Queenie was bad. Reddish-blonde dreads hung to the middle of her back, dark chocolate skin, chinky eyes, high cheek bones, full lips, nice teeth.

"My nigga just got out," Deso said, looking at Pop. "Give him some pussy."

A GANGSTER'S CODE

She mugged Deso again, and then Pop Somethin'. "Is you niggas crazy? Don't be wakin' me up for no fuck-shit. Leave me alone!"

Pop Somethin' took a couple steps toward the door. "I'm good, Deso. I ain't forcin' nobody to give up the pussy."

"Nah, Pop. It ain't like that. Hold on. She trippin'. Fuck yo' problem, Queenie? This my nigga, Pop Somethin'. He wit' the team. You know how we do."

When she heard his name, an apologetic look showed on her face. "You Pop Somethin'? For real?"

He noticed the change in her demeanor. "Yeah. I know you?"

"Nah, but I know who you is. Shit, e'erybody in Houston know who you is. Sorry for the attitude, but I was gettin' my beauty sleep. Damn, you big and sexy as fuck. When you get out?"

"Just now."

"I'm outta here, Pop. Do you," Deso said, leaving the room. Pop moved to close the door.

"You don't gotta close that. I mean, you can if you want, but it don't matter. We do what we wanna do 'round here, whenever we want to do it. We ain't shy about shit," Queenie said. And to prove her point, she climbed from under the sheet and stood up to let him see what she was workin' with. She wasn't wearing any clothes, so Pop checked her out. She was short and thick, big titties with large, black areolas, flat stomach, small waist, wide hips. She had tattoos from her neck to her ankles and an ass that made Pop's dick jump.

"This might take some getting used to," Pop chuckled, staring at her ass.

51

"Don't worry about it, baby. We got time. Get in the bed. Take yo' clothes off."

Pop Somethin' stripped like he was in a race to see who could get naked the fastest. Queenie walked to the dresser to grab a pack of condoms.

"Damn, nigga! Look at all those muscles. You sexy as fuck."

"I work out a li'l bit," Pop laughed. "What about her? She ain't gon' trip if she get woke up?"

"Nah. She prolly won't wake up. She fuck wit' dem pills, and they be havin' her ass out. But fuck her. She good. I want some dick. If she wake up and see yo' sexy ass, she gon' want some, too."

Pop Somethin' lay back, puffing the blunt while Queenie attacked his dick. She slurped on him like it was a popsicle, deep throating as much as she could. What she couldn't fit in her mouth, she jerked with her hand. She gagged and slobbered as she went to work. Pop grunted and moaned as she slayed his dragon. His nut built up quick. It had been eight years. He tried to hold off, but couldn't.

"Ooh, shit!" he grunted, feeling lightheaded.

Queenie looked him in his eyes as she pumped the nut out of him, sucking him dry. When she was done, she kissed the head of his dick and smiled. "And you still hard. How you want it, Daddy?"

Pop took another puff on the blunt. She was so sexy, and her ass was so fat. "Face down, ass up."

After putting on the rubber, Queenie assumed the position. He got behind her and slipped in slowly. She was hot and wet. It felt like he was about to bust again, so he paused.

"Nuh-uh, nigga. Fuck me hard!" Queenie said, slapping her ass.

While he was locked up, Pop Somethin' read that if you thought about bullshit while you fucked, you could last longer, so he thought about all kind of sports as he dug her guts out.

"Oh, hell yeah, nigga. I'ma fall in love wit' cho dick!"

Pop continued puffing the blunt as he fucked her. She didn't even notice when the ashes fell on her ass, just kept throwing it back at him and moaning his name. He held off the second nut for as long as he could. After he busted, Queenie changed his rubber and climbed on top.

"Suck my titties," she told him as she rode the pipe.

Pop slapped ass and sucked her nipples as she went to work. Queenie was a real freak. She talked shit and cursed while she put the pussy on Pop. She started playing with her clit, too, then she came. She continued riding through her orgasm and didn't stop 'til Pop busted his third nut. When done, Queenie lay next to him, rubbing his body.

"Damn, I can't believe we just fucked. You know you a fuckin' legend, Pop?"

"People keep tellin' me that."

"I was twelve when you got locked up, but I remember how you had niggas shook. A nigga wit' that kinda power is an aphrodisiac. Get the pussy wet."

Pop laughed. "You wild, shawty. You sure yo' sister a'ight? We fucked good, and she didn't move."

"That's that pillhead sleep. She good. Bet if you start fuckin' her she wake up."

"Nah. I just ain't neva seen no shit like that."

"Don't trip. She good. But what up wit' chu? You gotta bitch?

Pop smirked. "What kinda question is that?"

"A real question. You just got out. Was a bitch holdin' you down, or do you need a bitch?"

"We fucked one time, and now you wanna be my woman?"

"I didn't say yo' woman or girl. I said yo' bitch. I know how niggas is out here. I ain't stupid. But if you need somebody to ride wit' chu or ride for you, I'm yo' bitch."

The look in her eyes told Pop she would worship him. Whatever business he needed handled, she would do his bidding. But he had a problem trusting strangers. "How you wanna ride wit' me and you don't even know me? What about dem niggas in the living room? They say you part of they team. Pop Squad."

"Is you with the team?"

"Nah. Deso my nigga, but I don't know them other niggas. Or nobody that's down wit' 'em."

"We call ourselves Pop Squad. Four niggas and four bitches. Deso named the team after you. He told us how real you was, and you was his mentor before you got locked up. Kept him fed and showed him how to hit niggas. He showed us the game, and now we all eat and sleep together."

Pop knew Deso started Pop Squad, but he didn't know the depths of the clique. He also didn't want to be a part of it. He trusted Deso, but he didn't know or trust anybody else, and he couldn't eat with niggas he didn't trust. "I ain't trynna come between what y'all got goin' on. It seem like a happy family. I just did eight years because I got set up by a nigga I thought was all the way down wit' me. I don't hand out my trust. That shit earned. I don't know yo' niggas, so I can't eat wit' em."

A GANGSTER'S CODE

"And that's why I wanna fuck wit' chu. We burnin' up H-Town. If I stay wit' Pop Squad, I'ma die or go to jail. I ain't scared of either. Shit, when it's my time, I won't cry. But I wanna see more and do more. You not fuckin' wit' us tell me you got cho own plans. You smarter than Deso an' 'em. He wanna be like you. He yo' shadow. You the real thing. Why would I stay fuckin' the shift manager when I can fuck wit' the boss?"

J-BLUNT

Chapter 6

"Deso, I need some heat," Pop Somethin' said, sliding into his t-shirt as he walked into the living room.

"What you want? Choppers? Pistols?"

"Shit, lemme get a chopper."

Drama pulled a black AR-15 from under the couch. "This bitch got two fifty-round clips. You need more than that?"

Pop Somethin' took the gun, staring at it like he had fallen in love. "Nah. This bitch is perfect."

"So, what the move? You need the team?" Deso asked.

"Nah. Me and Queenie got this. Is it cool if she fuck wit' me? She don't got no obligations, do she?"

"Shit, y'all both Pop Squad. Whatever you need her to do, she gon' do it."

"Look, Deso, you my nigga. I fuck wit' chu the long way, but I ain't wit' this Pop Squad shit. I got my own plans. Once I finish doin' what I gotta do, I'm movin' outta town."

Deso looked hurt. "I did this for you, my nigga. Put a squad together so we can get down like we used to."

"No disrespect, but these yo' niggas. I can't jump into nothin' blind. I don't know what kinda shit y'all in or who y'all beefin' wit'. I'm solo for now."

"What kinda shit is that, dawg?" Yea spoke up. "You think we fake? Nigga, we put in work!"

Pop mugged Yea. "But I don't know you, nigga. And I don't eat wit' niggas I don't know."

"Nigga, that shit sound slick as a bitch. While you was in a box, we was puttin' niggas in boxes," Yea spat.

"Get cho boy, Deso," Pop warned.

"Chill, Yea. Get off that fuck shit! This my nigga."

"Man, I ain't trynna hear none of dat'. Nigga come in here actin' like he Jesus. He don't wanna eat wit' us, and he trynna split the team. I don't give a fuck who this nigga is. Nigga gon' respect my gangsta."

"Yea, calm down, nigga! I just told yo' ass to chill!" Deso barked.

While the Pop Squad went back and forth, Pop Somethin' checked the AR. When he cocked the machine gun, the room got quiet. Pop pointed the gun at Yea and squeezed the trigger. Twice. One bullet hit him in the chest, the other in the neck. Yea choked on blood as he struggled to breathe. Drama, Snot, and Deso looked back and forth from Pop Somethin' to Yea. Nobody moved or said a word.

"Damn. This bitch ain't no ho," Pop laughed, watching Yea die slowly.

"Pop! What the fuck, nigga?" Deso yelled.

"You hear how reckless that nigga's lips got? Only reason I gave him the first pass was 'cause he yo' boy. You know I don't fuck around."

Queenie ran into the living room. "What happened? Who shootin' in the house?" She stopped when she seen Yea dead on the couch and Pop Somethin' holding the gun. "What happened?"

"Judgment. You ready?"

She looked at the other Pop Squad members. They wore shocked and surprised looks on their faces. "Damn. You don't play. Shit."

"You see how I move. What it's gon' be?"

She looked at Deso one more time. He looked stuck. Then she turned back to Pop Somethin'. "You got another gun?"

A GANGSTER'S CODE

Pop smiled and gave her the Glock 40 he got from Smoke. Then he turned to Deso. "We good, bruh?"

Deso looked at Yea's dead body, then back at Pop. "Yeah. Nigga talked his way into that one. Damn, I wish you woulda gave the nigga a pass."

"Passes is for football players. I play for keeps."

***

After parking the Infinity at the curb, Pop Somethin' turned to Queenie. "Tell me more about you? How you start fuckin' wit' Deso an' 'em?"

"Trynna get money. Deso got a baby wit' my homegirl, Emmy. Once she told me how they be robbin' niggas for ten or twenty Gs, I was in. Dancers live fast, and we run into a lot of niggas wit' money. Deso an' 'em do all the work. We lure niggas, and they hit 'em"

"You eva have to get down on a nigga?"

"Once. A nigga got the ups on Deso and Drama, so I shot him. He didn't die. I hit him in the stomach."

"How you feel about what I did to Yea?"

"I mean, he Pop Squad. But at the same time, you Pop Somethin'. If he was talkin' shit, he got what he had comin'."

"You think the rest of them niggas feel the same way?"

"Deso, maybe, 'cause y'all boys. But Drama and Snot might not let that shit go. I think they might try to get at you."

"Yeah. I think the same thing. So, where yo' loyalty at?"

"Wit' chu and my sister."

"Yo' sister still Pop Squad. What if she roll wit her niggas against me?"

"She won't. Me and my sister got a special bond."

Pop raised an eyebrow. "What that mean?"

"You gon' see when the time right. Look. Somebody leavin' the house."

A man and a woman walked off the porch of a black-and white brick house. They were oblivious to the wolves that lurked in the silver Infinity. The couple hopped into a white BMW and drove away.

"Was that him?" Queenie asked.

"Nah. That was his brother. It's on you now. You sure you ready? This a trial by fire, and I play for keeps."

She leaned over and gave him a long tongue kiss. "Watch me, baby. I'ma blink the lights twice when I'm ready for you." Queenie put an extra switch in her hips as she got out of the truck and walked up on the porch of the brick house. She was dressed in a body-hugging red cat suit, red bottom heels, and carried a Louis Vuitton clutch.

She didn't have to wait on the porch long after ringing the doorbell. "Who dat?" a man called from the house.

"I'm sorry to bother you. My name is Jessica. My car broke down, and I need help."

When the door opened, a tall, dark-skinned nigga eyed Queenie. "Who is you? What chu want?"

"Sorry, man. My name Jessica. My car broke down. Can I use your phone? I need to call my sister."

He eyed her body. The red and blonde dreads and the cat suit had her looking irresistible.

"Who at the door, baby?" a woman asked from in the house.

"Some chick Jessica. Said her car broke down and she need to use the phone."

A GANGSTER'S CODE

A pretty, brown-skinned woman with shoulder-length permed hair appeared at the man's side. After looking Queenie from head to toe, she gave her man a you-won't-be-helping-her look. "Go check on the baby. I got it."

He took one more look at Queenie before disappearing.

"C'mon in, girl. What happened?"

"My car broke down around the corner. Yo' neighbors so rude. They wouldn't even help me. I just need to use the phone to call my sister."

"Not everybody want a woman that got it goin' on like you in they house. You probably intimidated the whole block. Have a seat. I'ma grab my phone from the other room."

When the woman left, Queenie found the light switch and flipped it twice. When the woman came back into the living room, her mouth dropped open. Queenie had the Glock 40 pointed at her chest.

"Don't scream, bitch! Open the front door."

She did as she was told. Pop Somethin' walked in carrying the AR-15.

"Where he at?"

Queenie looked at the woman. "I don't know. Ask her."

"Where yo' man at? How many people in the house?"

"Just me, my man, and our baby. Please don't hurt us. You can have whatever you want."

"Take me to yo' man."

He was in the bedroom, sitting on the couch with his one-year-old son in his arms. When his wife walked into the room, he immediately noticed the tears in her eyes and look of terror on her face. "What's goin' on, baby? Where that lady?"

He stopped talking when Queenie and Pop Somethin' walked into the room with their guns out. "You look like you just seen a ghost, Scarp," Pop Somethin' sneered.

"P-Pop Somethin'. Shit. Uh, c-c'mon, dawg. Let's talk about dis."

"Talk, nigga. I'm listenin'."

"Um. J-Just tell me how to make it right. I got money. What chu want?"

"All of it."

"I-I got a safe in the closet. Eighty Gs. That's you."

Pop looked at Queenie. "Check it out."

On the top shelf was a small safe. Next to it was a silver revolver. She gave the gun to Pop Somethin' and sat the safe on the bed.

"Open it, nigga," Pop ordered.

Scrap lay the baby on the bed and nervously fumbled with the combination. When it was open, he looked up at Pop Somethin' with hope in his eyes. "Eighty Gs. It's all you."

Pop Somethin' smiled. "Good lookin'. But I know you didn't think that shit was gon' be this easy. You tried to kill me, nigga. I still got cho bullet in my back."

"C'mon, Pop."

"Shut the fuck up, nigga! It's over. You dead!

Scrap and his wife cried while Pop Somethin' emptied the bullets from the revolver. It was a 38 Special. Pop put one bullet back in the gun and held it out to Scrap's wife. "One of 'em gotta die. Yo' baby or Scrap. You choose."

Crocodile tears fell from the woman's eyes. "Please don't make me do this. I don't know what he did to you, but I'm sorry. Take the money. We can get more if you want. Please don't do this."

"Listen, bitch. That nigga tried to kill me. If you wanna live, you betta kill his ass. This my last offer. Take this gun and kill one or I'ma kill all y'all."

She sobbed like a child as she took the gun. Scrap cried with her. After some hesitation, she pointed the gun at her husband. Her body shook as she tried to pull the trigger. "I can't do it," she cried.

"Go 'head, baby. Do it. I fucked up. This the way it gotta be," Scrap encouraged.

"I can't. I love you."

"You gotta do it, or he gon' kill you and li'l Brian. Do it. I love you."

Pow!

The bullet went through Scrap's forehead, exploding out the back and leaving his brains on the wall. His wife collapsed to her knees, crying. When the baby started crying, Pop Somethin' grabbed a pillow and smashed it onto the boy's face.

"No!" the woman cried, jumping to her feet and rushing Pop Somethin'.

Pop!

The woman fell onto the bed next to Scrap, a hole the size of a quarter in the back of her head. Queenie stood over her, eyes wide, breathing shallow, holding a smoking 40 Glock.

"You a'ight?" Pop Somethin' asked, removing the pillow from the dead child's face after a minute or two and breathing somewhat heavily.

A bewildered look came over Queenie's face as she looked from all the dead bodies to Pop Somethin'. "Damn, Pop. I feel," she paused to search for the words. "Strange. Powerful. Like I can do anything."

"You did good, girl. We bound by blood now. It's me and you against the world. You my queen. I'm yo' king."

She responded by walking over to Pop Somethin' and kissing him. "Damn, Pop. I ain't neva felt like this before. I feel like a god. My pussy so wet. Feel it."

After a struggle to get the cat suit down, Pop stuck his finger into her pussy and tasted her juices. "Damn. Murda get my bitch wet. You a freak!"

"C'mon, Pop. I'm horny. Fuck me real quick," Queenie said, kneeling on the bed next to the dead family.

Pop laid the AR-15 on the dead baby and unzipped his pants. Queenie's pussy was hot and wet. He slipped in easily. She moaned his name and threw her ass back at him while he fucked her. Earlier he fucked her with a condom and her pussy was good. Now that he was in her raw, her pussy was so good he wanted to fuck her forever.

Forever came quicker than he wanted it to. It only took a few minutes for him to bust.

"Damn, we some freaks, girl," he laughed, zipping his pants.

Queenie wore a satisfied look as she pulled up her clothes. "That shit was fire, baby. Best sex I ever had."

"Speakin' of fire, grab that safe and get to the truck. I'ma be out right after I set this bitch on fire."

Chapter 7

Pop Somethin' was normally a light sleeper. In prison he had to be. His life could have depended on it. But on his second day of freedom, the soft hotel mattress had him in a deep slumber.

Queenie got up to use the bathroom. After washing her hands, she stood in the bathroom doorway listening to Pop Somethin's light snore. In one day her life had changed. She had gone from being a stripper running with a clique of jack boys to a murderess, bound by the blood of victims to a street legend with a quick temper. She hadn't had the time to stop and think about what she had done until that moment. She had killed, taken a life, helped set a family on fire. And she felt powerful. Like a goddess. Pop Somethin' had awakened something deep within, something she never knew existed, and now that the monster had been released from its cage, she wanted to spill more blood. Taste more death. Feel more power.

The thought of murder made her pussy tingle. She noticed the tent Pop Somethin's morning hardness made under the sheet. She went to him, peeling the covers back, exposing his chiseled body. She used her mouth to make love to him, taking her time, sucking, licking, and kissing his dick. Pop Somethin' moaned as he stirred. His hands found the back of her head, guiding her. She kept sucking him, getting lost in her own zone. When he busted his nut, she swallowed it all, not wasting a drop.

"G'mornin', Pop. How you feel?"

He smiled. "Like a boss, man."

"I'm glad. Now lay back so I can bounce on yo' dick and get mine."

Pop lay back as Queenie put a rubber on him and climbed on top. She started off slow, running her hands through her dreads. Pop Somethin' reached out and began squeezing her nipples as she rode him. Queenie moaned her approval, speeding up her pace, her orgasm building fast.

"Pull on my nipples," she told Pop.

He did, tugging her nipples roughly. Queenie loved it. She tilted her head back, screaming his name as she came.

After another round of sex in the shower, Pop Somethin' and Queenie hit the mall for a change of clothes and then hopped on the highway. Several hours later the GPS guided them to the curb of a red, white, and blue house in Fort Worth, Texas.

"What if she not here? Why didn't you call her first?" Queenie asked.

"She here. I know her schedule. Her bum-ass nigga make sure she don't got no life."

"You don't sound like you feelin' her man. Who is he?"

"I don't know, but I hope he here so I can find out."

Pop Somethin' tucked the Glock 40 in his waist and Queenie hid the 38 Special in her clutch. When they were decent, the couple left the truck and walked up to the house. Pop Somethin' rang the doorbell.

"Who is it?" a female called.

"Pop. Open the door, girl."

When the door flew open, Shanice ran out and jumped into Pop's arms. "What's up, cousin? Welcome home! Why didn't you call me?"

"'Cause I wanted to surprise you. Surprise!"

Queenie stood off to the side and watched the cousins have a love fest. Shanice hugged him tightly and kissed him on the cheek several times. "I'm jealous," Queenie joked.

Shanice looked at Queenie as she climbed from Pop's arms. "I'm sorry. I'm so rude. Hi. I'm Shanice, his cousin. Are y'all together?"

"I know who you are. He told me all about you. I was just playin' about bein' jealous. I'm Queenie."

After exchanging smiles, Shanice turned to Pop Somethin'. "You didn't tell me you had a girlfriend, cousin."

"She not my girl. She my bitch."

Shanice looked surprised and didn't know what to say. Queenie spoke up. "It's cool. It is what it is. He my nigga. I'm his bitch. Bonnie and Clyde, ride-or-die shit."

"Oh. Okay. If you like it, I love it. Y'all come in. Damn, cousin, you huge! What was you eatin' up in there?"

"Everything," Pop Somethin' said, sniffing the air as he walked into the house. "I'm hungry. What you got to eat?"

"You right on time. I was just making us dinner. Meatloaf, mashed potatoes, cornbread, and glazed carrots. Come in the kitchen. I'm feeding Shawntale."

The smell of food made Pop Somethin's stomach growl. After the long drive he was starved, and the smells from the kitchen had him feeling weak.

When the big man walked in the kitchen, the little girl sitting at the table stopped eating and her eyes popped.

"Pop, this is my daughter, Shawntale. Shawntale, say hi to cousin Pop," Shanice said.

The toddler just stared at him with a wide-eyed gaze.

"Hi, Shawntale," Pop waved.

The child didn't speak. She just stared at the intimidating giant.

"I don't know what's wrong with her. Yo' li'l t-shirt and muscles got her tongue-tied. Sit down. I'ma make y'all some plates," Shanice said as she went over to the stove.

Pop p pulled up a chair next to Shawntale. "She cute as fuck. Look just like you when you was little. She just gotta warm up to me. All ladies love Pop Somethin'. Ain't that right, Queenie?"

Queenie rolled her eyes. "Stop, Pop. You doin' too much. But she is a li'l cutie. Look like you spit her out, Shanice. Make me want a mini-me."

Pop Somethin' mugged Queenie. "Quit playin'."

"Chill, Pop. I'm twenty. I don't want no kids right now. I'm young and havin' fun."

"Kids might not be a bad thing for you, cousin," Shanice said as she sat plates of food in front of Queenie and Pop. "They might help you calm down, help you change."

"I don't need changing. The world need more niggas like me. And stop plantin' seeds in my bitch's head. We don't need no babies. We good."

"She ain't plantin' no seeds, baby. Believe me," Queenie said, digging into the meatloaf. "Damn, girl. You can burn!"

"I got a baby and a man that ain't neva satisfied. Sunny Anderson taught me a few things."

"This shit is fiya!" Pop mumbled in between bites. "Where yo' man at, anyway? I wanna meet him."

"I don't know. In the streets. He comes and goes."

"He don't got no job?"

"Nope. He get his money the best way he know how."

"You remember what I used to tell you about street niggas? Niggas ain't shit. But you fucked around and got wit' one anyway. Street niggas don't know how to do that family shit."

"C'mon, Pop. Niggas in suits and ties with college degrees don't come around the hood. I'm attracted to what I see."

"They be around. You just wasn't lookin' hard enough."

"C'mon, cousin. We not about to dissect my love life."

He brushed off her words. "Lemme get anotha piece of meatloaf. And yeah, we is about to dissect yo' love life. Since you wouldn't tell me about yo' nigga while I was locked up, you gon' tell me now."

Shanice grabbed the pan of meatloaf and sat it on the table. "Can't we just kick it and chill? I got some wine."

"You know I don't drink."

"I do," Queenie spoke up.

Shanice got up to pour her and Queenie glasses of white wine. "So, what you finna do, Pop? Where are you living?"

"I don't know yet. I'm s'posed to fuck wit' C-Note in Dallas. You heard from him lately?"

"Yeah. He texted me the other day. He cool."

"Do that nigga be puttin' his hands on you?" Pop asked, taking half the pan of meatloaf on his plate.

Shanice frowned. "You talkin' 'bout C-Note?"

Pop Somethin' mugged hers "Stop playin'. You know who I'm talkin' 'bout."

"Sometimes, yeah. We fight like everybody else. Don't eat all the meatloaf. Save some for Nitty. I don't wanna hear his mouth."

"Fuck that nigga."

"C'mon, Pop. Don't –"

The front door opening made everybody pause. Shanice looked nervous. Pop Somethin' smiled.

"Shanice! Shanice! Who's truck is that parked in front of the house?" Nitty screamed.

"It's my cousin's. We in the kitchen."

When Nitty stumbled into the kitchen, he immediately noticed Pop Somethin'. The street legend looked like a giant sitting next to Shawntale. When they locked eyes, Pop smiled. "'Sup, nigga?

Nitty looked at Shanice. "Who dis nigga?"

"This my cousin, Pop Somethin'. He just got out."

Nitty's eyes lit up. "Oh shit! You the nigga I been hearin' all that shit about."

Pop sneered. "Funny thang is, I never heard shit about you. But cho girl can cook the fuck outta some meatloaf," he said, digging into the pan and putting another big piece of meatloaf on his plate. The tiny piece he left behind was barely enough to satisfy Shawntale.

Nitty looked at the small portion, and then at Shanice. "Where my plate?"

Shanice looked at the almost empty pan of meat and then back to Nitty. A scared look flashed across her face. "I told him not to eat it all. I'm sorry, baby. Pop Somethin', why you do that?"

Pop eyed Nitty as he put a big chunk of meat in his mouth and chewed like he was on a food commercial. "I was hungry. Shit is fine as a muthafucka. You need to taste this shit, bruh."

Queenie sat her fork down and reached for her clutch.

Nitty clenched his fist, his face scrunched. "Nigga, I know you just didn't eat all my food!"

A GANGSTER'S CODE

Pop sat the fork down and rubbed his stomach. "Damn. I guess I did. I prolly shouldn'ta did that, huh?"

"Bitch-ass nigga! I'ma fuck you up!" Nitty screamed.

Queenie reacted quickly, pulling the revolver from her purse. Before she could point it at Nitty, Pop Somethin' was on his feet. He moved with the speed and power of a lion about to kill. Nitty was a big man, six-foot-two and 220 pounds, but Pop Somethin' was bigger and faster. His left hand was a blur, tapping Nitty on the nose and making his neck snap back. The right that followed crashed into his jaw.

Nitty's feet flew from under him like he stepped on a wet spot. Blood flowed from his nose as he stared up at the ceiling. Shawntale and Shanice cried in the background.

Pop Somethin' knelt over Nitty, slapping him a couple times to wake him up. "Nitty! Aye, Nitty! Can you hear me? If you put cho hands on my cousin again, I'ma kill you. This yo' only warning."

J-BLUNT

Chapter 8

"Damn, nigga! I forgot how big yo' ass was," C-Note said as he hugged Pop Somethin'.

"What's good, li'l nigga? I see you eatin' good out here. You wasn't jackin', huh?"

"I told you I was about to run it up out here. These my niggas Artie and Lucci, the one that can't handle his liquor."

Pop Somethin' acknowledged them with a nod. They were gathered at Spin City, the strip club C-Note had come to know as his second home.

"Fuck you, nigga. I can handle my liquor," Lucci said, falling into his chair.

"Who is yo' girl?" C-Note asked, eyeing Queenie. The chocolate beauty had let her hair down, the gold and red dreads flowing down her back. The black body suit flexed around her killer curves, and the red bottoms made her ass sit in the air like a bubble.

"Don't look at her like that, dawg. You can't handle her," Pop joked. "This my bitch, Queenie. She move wit' me on all levels."

"What up, baby?" Queenie smiled, licking her lips.

C-Note nodded. "Y'all have a seat. Want a drink?" he asked, gesturing to the table filled with bottles of top-shelf liquor.

"I don't drink," Pop said.

Queenie reached for the bottle of Hennessy. "I want some dark tonight."

"You don't drink, bruh?" Lucci asked, looking at Pop like he was from a different planet.

"Nah. That shit be havin' niggas slippin'. Like you."

"I ain't slippin', nigga. I'm turnt!" Lucci laughed, smacking a nearby stripper on the ass.

Pop Somethin' shook his head, blowing Lucci off and turning to C-Note. "So, what chu doin' out here, li'l bruh? What kinda shit you trynna get me into?"

"Basically, my nigga, I want you to be my security. Be my shooter. I got fifty Gs for you. Do whatever you wanna do wit' it. I'm out here eatin' and niggas be hatin'. I want you to watch my ass. put in work when it need to be done."

"That's it? For real?"

"Yeah."

"So what, this s'posed to be a contract? I ain't never had a nigga approach me wit' no shit like this before. I normally just take a nigga shit. And for my niggas, I put in work for free. Outta love."

"This different. Ain't no contracts. Just be wit' the squad. Fuck wit' us. Too many niggas locked up for lookin' out. It's 'bout that paper. I got clean heats If you need 'em. That fifty is for you to get on yo' feet. Let me know if you need more. I'm still throwin' parties and runnin' it up on the highways. Big risks equal big rewards. We also renovating a building to turn it into a strip club. Want it to open in a couple months. It would be nice if she could open it up," he explained, looking at Queenie.

"Cool wit' me," Pop said.

"If I can be the featured dancer, I'm in," Queenie said.

C-Note agreed. "Say no more."

"We need to get her, too," Artie said, nodding toward the main stage. Skittlez was entertaining the crowd, twerking while doing a handstand.

"She good. And she bad," Queenie said, noticing how Skittlez worked the crowd.

A GANGSTER'S CODE

"That nigga Franco be havin' that bitch," C-Note said.

Lucci nodded toward the door. "Speakin' of a bitch-nigga."

ABLE Team mobbed into the strip club twenty deep. Franco led the pack, Radar by his side. They walked through the club like red carpet had been laid out. Security escorted them to a champagne room. During the walk, C-Note and Franco exchanged hostile looks.

"'Sup wit' them niggas?" Pop Somethin' asked.

"That's the competition, ABLE Team. I'm puttin' a dent in them niggas' pockets, and they hatin'. Plus, that nigga runnin' 'round sayin' I robbed him."

"Did you?"

C-Note laughed. "Yeah. When that nigga was outta town. We ran in on his bitch. Ain't looked back since."

Pop Somethin' smiled like a proud father. "Damn, li'l nigga. I had you all wrong. I see you get down for yours."

"When it comes to checkin' a bag, I get it. That shit you niggas was on in the pen was too much for me. But out here, I go hard in the paint."

"I respect that. But back to these ABLE Team niggas. Y'all wore masks when y'all did the hit?"

"Nah. We was in and out quick."

"You know that shit can come back and bite you in the ass? Leavin' witnesses gets a lot of niggas fucked. I'm doin' 'em all in. Shorties, too."

"It's been a minute since that shit happened. Them hos was too scared to remember us."

Pop Somethin' gave him a look. "A'ight."

"Excuse me, baby. I'ma go have a word wit' the DJ," Queenie said, standing to her feet. Skittlez had just come off the stage, and Queenie was eyeing her.

"What you on?" Pop asked, noticing the mischievous look on his bitch's face.

"It ain't safe. It ain't safe. It ain't safe. It ain't safe," she sang.

The deep voice on the microphone got everybody in the club's attention. "Check this out! Check this out! I neva had this happen before. I need to get everybody attention. I got a special, fine, and sexy thang next to me that say she wanna put on a show. I neva seen her before, but as y'all can see, she bad. And she ain't shy. And the most important thang is she want, our girl Skittlez to help her do the show. I'm tellin' y'all this 'cause I need y'all to dig in y'all pockets and make it thunderstorm in this bitch!"

After the DJ made the announcement, all eyes in the club flocked to Skittlez and Queenie. Skittlez's light skin and Queenie's dark skin looked like they could make magic happen if they blended. Dollar signs flashed in Skittlez eyes as she turned to Franco. Whenever he was in the club, she gave him all of her attention, but not tonight.

"Lemme catch a check real quick, baby."

Franco wanted to protest the show. He knew Queenie was at the table with C-Note, and he didn't want nobody connected to him to make moves with his competition, but the one thing he knew he couldn't do was try to get between a stripper and her money, so he told her, "Shut it down, gurl."

Skittlez wore a red bra, orange lace panties, and green heels. Her ensemble, along with her yellow skin, pink hair, and purple nails had her looking like a bag of candy. "C-mon, Zane," she said, turning to the DJ. "Give her a bottle of that oil."

A GANGSTER'S CODE

The DJ handed Queenie a bottle of baby oil as she walked up on the stage. She was still dressed in the black cat suit, but she didn't need to be naked for everybody to know she was strapped. Queenie and Skittlez stood face-to-face, eyeing each other sexually. Cardi B's *Bodak Yellow* brought their bodies to life. Queenie walked to the edge of the stage and showed the crowd she could bounce one ass cheek at a time. When they made noise, she dropped to her knees and shook it all around.

Skittlez joined her, pressing their asses together and bouncing them to the same rhythm.

The baby oil was used on Skittlez first. Queenie sprayed it all over her body and rubbed it into her light-skinned flesh. When she was good and oiled up, Skittlez made her glistening backside clap for the crowd. Queenie slapped her ass cheeks as they bounced.

When the song changed, so did the main attraction. Queenie was stark naked underneath the cat suit. Colorful tattoos covered her dark skin from head to toe. Big, perky breasts, dark chocolate areolas, and thick thighs had the crowd in a trance. She danced to Nikki Minaj and Yo Gotti's *Rake it Up*. Skittlez sprayed the dark-skinned beauty with baby oil as they re-enacted the infamous *Tip Drill* video.

The women slipped around on the stage for ten minutes, and niggas made it rain to show their appreciation. When they were done, so much money was on the stage they gathered it in two garbage bags. While they were in the back showering, Queenie took her shot at Skittlez.

"I like the way you put on a show. That shit was hot as fuck."

"That was all you, baby. Yo' thick, chocolate ass had them niggas goin' crazy," Skittlez laughed.

"It's all about a check, gurl. I knew me and yo' bad ass would have niggas cashin' out. When I see somethin' I like, I make my move."

Skittlez quoted BeyoRee. "'A diva is a female version of a hustla.'"

"Preach, bitch!" Queenie laughed, giving a little bounce.

"So, what chu doin' for the rest of the night? I got a place we can chill."

Skittlez thought about Franco. When he came to the club, most nights she left with him. He paid well. But there was something about her new dark-skinned friend that made her mind wonder. She had fucked, danced with, and got money with plenty of women, but Queenie's look and vibe was making Skittlez rethink where she would spend the night. "Who is the tall nigga you with? I never seen him with C-Note before."

"That's my nigga, Pop Somethin'. We new in the city. We from H-Town. We stayin' in a suite 'til we find a place to settle down at."

"Did you know C-Note and ABLE Team wasn't seein' eye-to-eye? If I leave witcha all, Franco might feel some type of way."

"I say throw the cards in the air and let 'em fall. Franco ain't cho man, is he? We young, bad, and got money. Sometimes you gotta do what make you feel good."

***

Franco eyed Skittlez and Queenie as they walked out of the back dressing room in street clothes. He expected

Skittlez to walk over to him, but she didn't. She followed Queenie over toward C-Note's table.

"Skittlez! What's good, shawty?" he asked, raising his arms.

Skittlez spun around and gave him a smile and two-finger salute before leaving the club with Pop Somethin' and Queenie.

The women drank and freaked in the back of the Infinity. Pop Somethin' watched them in the rearview mirror, barely able to keep his eyes on the road. When they got to the hotel, he grabbed the duffle bag from the back of the truck. Inside was the eighty thousand they took from Scrap and the murder weapons. Tomorrow he would dispose of the guns and get new ones from C-Note. Tonight it was party time!

When they got in the room, they wasted no time getting naked. Drinks flowed, the women popped pills, and Pop Somethin' fired up the weed. He lay back on the bed, blowing smoke rings at the ceiling while Skittlez and Queenie kissed and took turns sucking his dick.

"Let me see this," Skittlez said, taking the blunt from Pop Somethin'. "Wanna see a trick?"

Pop Somethin' smiled. "Impress me."

Skittlez lay back on the bed and took a big puff on the blunt. After blowing out a cloud of smoke, she stuck the blunt between her legs, into her pussy. The cherry brightened as she used her vaginal muscles to puff the blunt.

Queenie crawled between her legs. "Gimme a shotgun."

Skittlez moaned as Queenie sucked the smoke out of her pussy. Then she lifted her head and blew out a cloud of smoke.

Pop Somethin' clapped his hands like he was watching a live play. "That shit was sexy as fuck," he grinned

"And her pussy taste so sweet, baby," Queenie said. "Come taste it."

Pop moved between Skittlez's legs and began licking her pearl. She grabbed ahold of his dreads, loving the feel of his tongue. Queenie watched them for a little while before getting in on the action. She crawled up Skittlez's body and sat on her face. Skittlez didn't waste time attacking Queenie's fat pussy. Curse words, moans, and screams of passion filled the air as the ménage à trois took off. Skittlez came first. Pop got up and went to Queenie, standing before her with his dick in her face. She took him into her mouth, sucking him hard as she continued to ride Skittlez's face. After Queenie came, they switched positions. Pop lay on his back, Queenie rode his dick, and Skittlez rode his face in reverse, tongue-kissing Queenie as they freaked. When Pop busted, they switched positions again: Skittlez face down, ass up and Queenie on her back with Skittlez's tongue in her pussy. Pop watched Skittlez eat Queenie for a few moments before putting on a rubber and sliding into Skittlez. Her yellow ass cheeks bounced violently as he beat the pussy up. When he was about to bust again, he snatched off the condom and began jacking off.

"Y'all come get this shit," he told the women.

They crawled over to him, waiting with their tongues out to catch his seed. When his nut finally came, he spread fluid back and forth in their open mouths, then used his dick to spread his seed across their faces.

"You bitches is bad," Pop laughed, watching them kiss and swap his sperm.

A GANGSTER'S CODE

***

"Damn, nigga. You been in town one day and you already stole my bitch," C-Note cracked.

"Bitches chase a good time and a check. I prolly did you a favor, nigga. Skittlez is a wild one."

"I'm fuckin' wit' chu, my nigga. That club is like my second home. I know how Skittlez get down. But fuck that bitch. I got them heaters for you in the bag on the back seat."

Pop looked over his shoulder and seen a duffel bag on the floor. He opened it and found two black, 50 caliber Desert Eagles with red beams, two Glocks with extended clips, an AK-47 with a fifty-round clip, and a bulletproof vest. He had gotten rid of all of his murder weapons earlier that morning, so the bag of guns was right on time.

"Damn. These muthafuckas makin' my dick hard," Pop admitted.

"You freak-ass nigga, dawg!" C-Note laughed. "I know a nice spot y'all can rent in a low-key neighborhood. My nigga Tank own some property. I'ma have him call you so y'all can get out that hotel."

"Bet. Bet. And what up wit' that fifty racks? I need to drop that in a safety deposit box before the bank close."

"We gon' grab it right after I make this run. This weak-ass bitch say she pregnant wit' my baby, and I need to stop by her sister house."

"Is it yours?"

"I don't know. Maybe. She just somethin' I was fuckin' on the side, but I hit it raw a couple times. I really been trynna duck the bitch, but since it's a possibility the shorty mine, I hit her wit' some paper every now and then."

81

"That shit sound messy, li'l bruh."

"It is what it is. I'ma be in and out real quick."

"A'ight. Lemme chill in the truck. Don't go in there and get no pussy and leave me out here for thirty minutes, nigga."

"I'm in and out, bruh," C-Note laughed.

C-Note parked the Audi truck in front of an apartment building that looked like a trap house, peeling paint, busted-out windows, and balding grass out front. When C-Note got out, Pop Somethin' began checking the guns. The DEs had four extra clips. The Glocks had thirty-shot extenders and a pair of twenty-one shot clips. He had just picked up the AK when he seen three niggas leave the apartment building across the street and go into the building C-Note went in. Pop Somethin' smiled as he grabbed the Desert Eagles. Before leaving the truck, he slipped on the bulletproof vest.

***

"Damn, nigga. I was wonderin' when you was gon' come see a bitch again," Deidra sassed, pressing her big titties into C-Note's stomach and chest as they hugged. Being four months pregnant caused her already enormous breasts to get even bigger.

"C'mon, shawty. You know I'm a busy man. Time is money."

"But I got cho baby. You don't fuck wit' Star no more. Why don't chu spend more time wit' me?"

"Because I just told you. Time is money. You changin' up now that you pregnant. You knew what it was from the jump. We was just kickin' it. I don't want no family."

"But chu got one. You shoulda thought about that before you started nuttin' in me."

C-Note seen the argument about to start, so he stopped it before it could begin. "Stop. We ain't finna go there. I told you we gon' see what happen when it's born. But I ain't gon' leave you fucked up. Here go a band."

She took the money eagerly, juggling her titties as she stuck the money in her bra. "Don't chu wanna spend some time wit' me? My sister at work, and I ain't had no dick in a minute."

"Not today, shawty. I just wanted to drop you some paper. I'ma get up wit' chu later."

Deidra looked like she wanted to cry. "For real, C-Note? That's it?"

"Yeah. I got some shit to do."

"You ain't shit! G'on get me pregnant then leave me all fucked up. You bogus, nigga," she pouted.

C-Note pulled her close and tried to soften her up. "C'mon, baby. Don't do this right now. I'ma get up wit' chu later. For real. Hit me later."

Deidra smiled, enjoying the affection. "You for real? You gon' come see me later?"

"Yeah. You know I keep my word. I brought you the money, didn't I?"

"Okay. Thank you, boo-boo. I'ma call you later."

After a hug and a quick peck on the lips, C-Note stepped into the hallway. He didn't see the goons until it was too late. They already had their guns out. All he could do was put his hands in the air.

"You know what dis is, nigga! We want the safe," one of them spoke as the other two searched him. They took thirty-five hundred dollars and a black 9 mm.

"That's all I got," C-Note said.

"Stop playin'. We know who you is, C-Note. We jumpin' in the Audi and goin' to yo' spot. Try some bullshit and I'ma bust yo' ass, nigga."

C-Note realized he had been set up. Deidra was a shysty bitch. But Pop Somethin' was outside. It was time to see what his fifty Gs had paid for.

He cooperated and they led him down a flight of stairs. They were almost at the front door when Pop Somethin' made his move. He had the element of surprise. Nobody expected him. The jackers were caught off guard as the Desert Eagles boomed. C-Note ducked. Two jackers went down with holes in their faces and chests. The third one got off a couple shots, hitting Pop Somethin' in the chest. He stumbled back and grimaced from the impact, but the vest absorbed the bullet. Pop quickly straightened up and gunned him down.

"What apartment that bitch in?" Pop barked, murder in his eyes.

"Upstairs. Apartment ten. But she might be pregnant wit' my seed," C-Note said.

"That bitch set chu up. That baby ain't yours. It's prolly one of them dead niggas' baby."

C-Note looked to the dead bodies lying on the floor. Deep down inside he knew Pop Somethin' was right. While the hired killa went upstairs to finish off the final witness, C-Note went to the truck.

When Pop Somethin' got to apartment ten, he didn't bother trying the door. He kicked it open and ran in. Deidra was nowhere to be found. He searched the house and found her in the bathtub, on the phone. Four .45 bullets to her face tore her shit apart.

Chapter 9

"Crist, when you go out, can you bring back some diapers and baby milk?" Carla asked.

C-Note ignored his sister as he stepped in front of the bathroom mirror to check his face. His haircut was fresh, facial hair trimmed, and a shower had him feeling so fresh and so clean. He had two meetings today, both of them important to his future.

More knocking on the door interrupted his thoughts. "Crist, I know you hear me. Trayvon need some diapers and milk."

C-Note snatched open the door and mugged his sister. "I heard you the first time. Damn. I got some shit to do. Call somebody and have them bring that shit. You got two baby daddies. Call one of them niggas."

Carla snarled her face. "You know I don't fuck wit' Rank, and I'm tired of Tray puttin' his hands on me. That's why I'm her wit' chu."

"Well, you gotta get somebody else to go to the store for you. I told you, I got shit to do."

Carla huffed and puffed as the siblings had a staredown. "Well, can you at least gimme some money to pay for it? I'ma give it back when I get my child support check."

C-Note shook his head as he grabbed his pants from his bathroom floor. After digging in his pockets, he shoved a hundred-dollar bill into Carla's hand. "Whateva, man. Keep that shit. Did you find you a house yet?"

"Nah. I'm still lookin'. I just need a li'l more time."

"A'ight. Do you need anything else? 'Cause I gotta get dressed and get out of here."

"Nah, we good. Thanks, bruh."

C-Note closed the bathroom door and finished freshening up. He loved his big sister, but damn, her and her three kids were getting on his nerves. They had taken over his house, and every time he turned around, Carla had her hand out, asking for money. He couldn't wait until she got her own shit again.

After getting dressed, he left the house and hopped into his silver E-Class Benz. He had gotten rid of the Audi truck after the episode at Deidra's sister's apartment building and now exclusively drove the Benz. When he pulled into the hotel's parking lot, he checked his phone again, re-reading the text. Room seven. His lucky number. After parking and taking a quick look around to make sure he wasn't followed, he found the room and walked in.

Sza's *The Weekend* crooned from a radio. The lights were turned off, but candles on the dresser and bedside table had the room glowing. Rose petals were on the floor and all over the bed. Shanice lay on the bed of roses, sucking an ice cube. She wore white lingerie and high heels, looking like she was posing for a sexy photo shoot. A bottle of champagne on ice sat on the floor at the foot of the bed.

"Damn, gurl! You sexy as a muthafucka!" C-Note said, pausing to stare at her.

"Why do it halfway? You make me feel special, and I want to return the favor. You just gon' stand there, or you gon' do somethin'? Don't you wanna know Victoria's secret?"

C-Note stripped out of his clothes and grabbed the bottle of Moet. While he drank from the bottle, Shanice grabbed her glass of champagne and crawled to the edge of the bed.

"You drinkin'? Don't you gotta go back to work?" he asked.

"I took the rest of the day off. "When me and Nitty fuck, he really just trynna get a nut. With you, I feel a special connection. I got a lotta pent-up sexual frustration I need to release. How much time you got?"

"However much time you need."

She grabbed his stick and stuck it in her glass of champagne. After using it to stir her drink, she sucked him into her mouth, staring into his eyes as she deep-throated him. A couple minutes later she dipped him into her glass again and sucked him some more. She kept at it 'til C-Note was ready to bust. When he was on the verge, she jacked him off, catching his cum in her glass. C-Note watched her swirl his thick, white seed in the liquor. Then she downed it like a shot.

"Mm. You taste good," Shanice said, licking her lips.

C-Note looked mesmerized. "Damn, gurl. You sexy as fuck!"

"How you gon' top that?" she challenged.

C-Note grabbed an ice cube from the bucket and popped it in his mouth. When Shanice lay back on the bed, he licked her from neck to feet. The hot and cold feel of the ice and his mouth made her moan in pleasure. When the cube melted, he grabbed another and pulled off her lingerie. Shanice shivered when he ran the ice across her nipples. When the ice melted again, he just sucked her nipples with his hot mouth. She ground her pussy against his torso. When she was good and hot, he grabbed another ice cube, popped it in his mouth, and stuck his face in her pussy. Shanice went wild! The hot and cold on her clit made her cum immediately. C-Note didn't stop. He used his tongue to push the ice in her pussy and then took his time sucking it out. Wave after wave of orgasm flowed through Shanice, making her body lock up. When he was done, all she could do was stare up at him, breathing like she had just run a race.

"Don't write no checks yo' pussy can't cash," he bragged.

Shanice smiled. "You did that, baby. But we ain't done yet. I told you I got some pent-up sexual frustrations"

C-Note crawled up her body and pinned her legs to her shoulders. After slipping his dick in, he paused, loving how tight and warm her pussy was. Then he beat it up. Shanice called his name and dug her nails into his skin as he fucked her. When they switched positions, she got on her knees and he got behind her.

"Pull my hair!" Shanice told him.

C-Note grabbed two hands of her shiny mane and fucked her. Shanice threw her ass back at him, using one hand to finger her clit and her other to massage his balls. C-Note slapped her ass and pulled her hair. Shanice busted first, crying out and shivering as the orgasm raced through her body. C-Note sped up, hitting it harder as his nut built up.

"Don't nut in me. Nut on me," Shanice told him.

When he was on the verge of erupting, C-Note pulled out his dick and began jacking off. Shanice flipped over and let him nut on her chest and stomach.

"Damn, girl. Yo' ass is a freak. Nitty stupid as fuck."

"I know. Now, don't you wanna take a shower with me and help me get clean? Or do you wanna lay here and talk about how stupid my baby daddy is?"

After another round of freaky-ass sex in the shower, they went back to the bed to chill. C-Note sipped champagne and smoked a blunt. Shanice didn't indulge since she had to pick up her daughter from the daycare in a couple hours.

"Yo' cousin crazy as fuck. You know that, right?" C-Note said, thinking about how Pop Somethin' saved his ass a couple days ago.

"Paul is a good nigga, but that temper got a lotta niggas put in the dirt."

"I neva met nobody like him. You think I can trust him?"

"Without a doubt. If he's with you, he's all the way with you. Just don't let him find out about us."

C-Note gave her a look. "You more worried about Nitty catching us, or Pop?"

"I'm worried about Nitty. You should be worried about Pop."

C-Note laughed. "You act like the nigga gon' kill me or somethin'."

Shanice didn't laugh.

"Damn. You serious? Why he so protective over you?"

"It's a long story. But basically, my daddy told him to watch out for me before he died. Pop Somethin' was there. They robbed a trap house. They almost got away, but somebody shot my daddy in the back while they was runnin' out the house. My daddy died in Pop Somethin's arms."

"Damn. When that happen?"

"Almost fifteen years ago."

"Damn. That's fucked up. But Pop only a couple years older than you, right? You sayin' he was robbin' traps when he was a li'l nigga?"

"Yeah. I'm twenty-four. He twenty-eight. My daddy took him under his wings early, right after he moved with us from Jamaica. They had some kinda war goin' on and his daddy died, so his momma sent him to live with us. He was seven or eight. My daddy and his daddy brothers. Pop basically worshipped our daddies. He was a wild child. Nobody could control him except our daddies. After my daddy died, I think he went crazy. Started robbin' and shootin' everybody. Had the whole city terrified. He was only twenty when he got locked up. Back then he was tall and skinny. Now he look like a monster with all those muscles, dreads, and that big-ass beard."

"That nigga is a monster!" C-Note said, replaying in his mind how easy and quickly Pop Somethin' killed. "So, I hooked up wit' a real killa, huh? You sure you wanna keep fuckin' around? I fuck wit' chu, Shanice, but I ain't trynna get on Pop bad side."

Shanice pushed C-Note onto his back and climbed on top of him. "You mean to tell me you can just walk away? Just like that?"

C-Note stared into her pretty face, getting lost in those seductive brown eyes. She was bad, and she had some good pussy, but she also had a crazy baby daddy and an even crazier cousin. He was stuck between a rock and a hard place. They had been fucking for five months. He was feeling her. If it wasn't for the crazy niggas in her life, he would've locked her down already. But as bad as he wanted to get out of bed and leave the hotel room, his desire to have as much of her time as possible outweighed rational thinking. "Damn, Shanice. You gon' get me killed."

A GANGSTER'S CODE

***

"Sergio, what's good, dawg?" C-Note smiled, giving the dark-skinned Puerto Rican a pound and half-hug. Nobody noticed, but C-Note could feel the small, metal key slipped into his palm.

"You got it, C-Note. Anytime I see you is a good thing." He smiled, revealing diamond and platinum teeth.

While the men talked, C-Note snuck a peek around the bus station to see if they were being watched. Everybody seemed to be minding their own business. "Same place?" he asked.

"You know it," Sergio smiled.

"When I'ma see Big Poppi? It's 'bout time I meet the man at the top. No disrespect, bruh, but I got big plans, and I need to discuss them with the big man."

He laughed. "C'mon, C-Note. You know the deal. Poppi don't play in the lake. He more of an ocean kind of fish. When the time is right, he'll see you. Don't rush progress. It's a slow process."

C-Note's spirit dampened a bit. He had high hopes on meeting the big man. When he met Sergio in prison, the Puerto Rican promised he had a connect on kilos for fifteen thousand. Turned out to be the real thing. They had only been doing business a short time, but C-Note was hustling good, and his money was constantly growing. Today he was buying twenty kilos. The transaction was always in a public place, mostly the bus station. He picked up from the lockers and dropped the money off in the back of the toilet.

"Yeah, I hear you, man. Check the first stall."

"Okay, homes. Be cool. Stay safe."

It didn't take C-Note long to find the locker. Number seven. This was the second time today he found goodies behind door number seven. A black girl behind the hotel door and 20 white girls behind the locker door.

After grabbing the duffel bag, he left the bus station and stepped out into the bright Dallas sunlight. Cars revving their engines and tires screeching got his attention. A black Charger with tinted windows had jumped the sidewalk. Next to it was a black Camaro. Four men with automatic weapons jumped out of the cars. They wore black military-style uniforms. Silver badges hung from their necks.

"Stay right there! Hands up! Don't move!" they yelled.

C-Note threw his hands high in the air, scared stiff. It was the DBA. The real alphabet boys. When the realization of what was happening registered in his mind, C-Note became panicked. Jail was hell for him. He couldn't go back. Be had only been out six months. He had big plans. It couldn't be over. Not like this.

"Get down on the ground!" they yelled.

The demanding voice snapped him from the trance he was in. The feds were surrounding him. He had to get rid of the dope. So he ran.

"Hey! Stop! Freeze!"

C-Note ignored the commands and ran for his life. Next to the bus terminal was a parking lot. That's where he ran. The feds gave chase. He ran past a bus being loaded with suitcases and threw the duffel bag in the pile and kept running. They continued to chase, gaining on him. Then his lungs began to burn. He knew he would be caught. The alphabet boys were in much better shape.

A GANGSTER'S CODE

About twenty yards later, a fed jumped onto his back, tackling him to the ground.

"Damn, C-Note. Why the fuck you make us chase you?" the agent breathed as he cuffed C-Note.

"'Cause y'all pulled guns on me. I ain't trynna get shot."

"You heard me tell you to stop. You seen the badges. That's how you get shot, moving when I say 'don't move.'"

"C'mon, man. Why you puttin' them cuffs on me? What y'all lookin' for me for?"

"Because you're a drug dealer. We're onto your boy, Big Papi. We don't want you or Sergio. We want the big fish. Cooperate with the state's attorney and you might walk."

"C'mon, man. I ain't no snitch."

"Yeah. That's what they all say."

***

Three days later

"You sure this it? I shouldn't even came and picked this nigga up. You know the feds take pictures and record everything. All our phones prolly tapped. Damn. I shoulda stayed home," Lucci vented.

"Chill, nigga. This our boy. If they was watchin' him, then they know who we is anyway, and they woulda got us, too. We good. All we gotta do is chill right here. He should be out in a minute," Artie said, relaxing in the passenger seat of the Jeep.

"I didn't even know the feds let you bail out. I thought once they had yo' ass, it was over."

"Me too. But I never got popped, so I don't really know. But here he go. Ask him."

C-Note climbed into the back of the SUV wearing a scared and nervous look. "What up, y'all? Good lookin' on pickin' me up."

"Fo' sho. You a'ight? Nigga, yo' ass look spooked," Artie laughed.

"Shit ain't funny, nigga. The feds on my ass. This shit is serious."

"So, how hot is you? How much they know?" Lucci asked.

"They wasn't on me. They want Big Papi. They know I'm a buyer. They want the big man."

"What that mean? They gon' drop yo' case? Since when the feds start givin' niggas bail?"

"They gotta give bail, nigga. Plus, I got a lawyer. I told you niggas to put up some money for a lawyer."

"So, what it look like?" Artie asked.

"I'm fucked. I got caught wit' twenty sparrows."

"You wanna fall back and lay low for a minute?"

C-Note paused, deep in thought. "Hell nah. I might be on my way back in. I gotta run it up and put some shit in order. We gotta turn it up and go harder."

Chapter 10

Two weeks later

Queenie rode Pop Somethin' reverse cowgirl, her face to the sky, head leaning backward. Pop held two handfuls of her dreads, tugging lightly. He matched her freak level in every way. He knew when to pull her hair, when to slap her ass, and when to choke her. The harder she rode him, the harder he pulled her hair. She could feel his body tensing up and knew he was about to bust. She had already gotten hers and was waiting for him to get his.

"Awe, shit! Damn, girl!" Pop groaned, filling her pussy with his seed.

Queenie slowed down, eventually coming to a stop. She spun to face him, keeping his dick inside as she leaned down for a kiss. "Damn, nigga. I think you got me dick-whipped. I ain't neva loved fuckin' a nigga as much as I love fuckin' you."

"That's 'cause you ain't neva met a nigga like me before."

"Preach, baby," she laughed. "So, what you doin' today? What's up wit' C-Note??

"I don't know. He been focused on the strip club openin'. I told him to take a step back. Them feds don't fuck around."

"Do you think he can beat the case?"

"Nah. Once them feds get you, it's a wrap. His best bet is to run it up out here and get his money right before he go in. He prolly finna be gone for a minute, unless he snitch and get a good deal."

"You think he will?"

"I can't say. I met the nigga while we was on lock. Niggas was extortin' him. He put me on for keepin' niggas off his ass. Based on that, he got a li'l bitch in him. But I don't know if it's enough to say he gon' snitch."

"I don't like it, Pop. I think we should make plans to leave. It sound like he done. Ain't no sense in us sinkin' wit' the ship."

Pop Somethin' became lost in his thoughts for a few moments. "I was thinkin' the same thing. The money is just so sweet that I didn't want to walk away. Ain't nobody never gave me fifty Gs to whack niggas. I did that shit for free. And I don't got a plan B."

"Well, what else do you want to do? What did you dream about while you was locked up?"

Pop smiled. "I always wanted to go back home."

"Back to Houston?"

"Nah, Jamaica. The island. I was born there."

Queenie was surprised. "For real? You Jamaican?"

"Yeah. Moms sent me to Houston after my pops died. I was six. They was havin' a big-ass war and she didn't want me to get caught up in it like my pops did. When I was locked up, I used to dream about goin' home wit' a million dollars, open up a hotel for tourists."

"Ooh! I never been to Jamaica. What is it like?"

"Some places is fucked up, but some is beautiful. My pops used to take me to this spot on the island called Eden. It had clear blue waterfalls. The grass and trees was so green and tall. The way the sunlight hit the clear blue water looked like some shit you see on postcards or vacation ads. I want to build my hotel on that spot. Not one of them big-ass chain hotels like the Hilton. Somethin' small. Call it Eden's Inn."

A GANGSTER'S CODE

"Damn, Pop. That shit sound amazing. I think you should do it."

"For real?"

"Hell yeah! I can see us on them beaches, fuckin' outside under the waterfall at Eden. My pussy gettin wet just thinkin' about it."

Pop Somethin' stared at her. "You would move to Jamaica wit' me? Just like that?"

"Yeah, you my nigga. I'm all the way down wit chu."

"What about yo' sister? What would the rest of yo' family say?"

"My sister the only family that matters, and she would be down to come, too."

Pop stared at her again. "A'ight. Fuck it. Let's do it. We chasin' a mil, baby."

"Damn, Pop! A million dollars. That shit gon' change our lives," Queenie said, blown away by thoughts of a million dollars and moving to Jamaica.

Pop' interrupted her thoughts. "What about you? What you dream of?"

She blushed and looked away. "Mine is stupid. I want to help you pursue yours."

"Stop playin', gurl. Tell me."

She took a moment to gather her courage. "Ever since I was little I wanted to get married and have a lot of kids and raise them and love 'em how they s'posed to be loved. Give them a good life like you see on TV. Momma and daddy in love, takin' kids to basketball and cheerleading practice, doin' family stuffs."

Pop laughed. "You serious? Damn. I wasn't expectin' that."

"I told you it was stupid."

"Nah, Queenie. It ain't stupid, I just wasn't expectin' you to say it. You don't seem like the motherly type. I remember what you was sayin' at Shanice house, but I thought you was just sayin' that in that moment. Where is all of this comin' from?"

She rolled off him and lay in bed. "I really don't wanna talk about it right now. Why don't we keep talkin' 'bout Jamaica and gettin' a mil?"

"'Cause I wanna know about you. Tell me."

Queenie's eyes found a spot on the wall that caught her attention. Then she opened up. "It was just me and Princess growin' up. Our daddy wasn't shit. He used to beat my momma ass and cheat on her. When we got older, we found out my momma was just his side bitch. The nigga had a whole other family on the other side of town. Married wit' kids. We grew up starvin' for attention from this nigga and he didn't give a fuck about us. Then my momma met this nigga, Chauncey. We thought he was gon' be our daddy, but when puberty hit, the nigga got touchy-feely. We told momma, but she didn't believe us until he raped Princess. But she blamed us. Said we was fast. Didn't even call the police. Chauncey was eventually fuckin' all three of us. When we turned sixteen, me and Princess found out about strip clubs. Been in the club ever since. That's why I want to have my own family, to give my kids the love, support, and stability I never had."

Pop was blown away. "Damn, baby. That shit was deep as fuck. Niggas ain't shit. Where that pussy-nigga Chauncey at? I wanna put his bitch-ass in the dirt."

"I don't know. I ain't seen him since we left home. Him and my momma stopped fuckin' around a long time ago. But if I ever see him, I'ma dead his ass."

A GANGSTER'S CODE

Silence filled the room as the couple became consumed by their individual thoughts. Queenie eventually broke it. "Pop, you the realest nigga I ever met. I never told nobody about my childhood. I feel safe with you. You bring out things in me I never knew existed."

He raised an eyebrow. "Like what?"

Queenie shifted. "Like murda. When I killed that bitch, I felt so powerful. Like a god. Like I could do anything. Sometimes I dream about killin' people. It gets my pussy wet. Am I crazy?"

"Nah, baby, you ain't crazy. You certified. I know exactly how you feel. Havin' power over who live or die get me geeked up, too. Shit, seein' some new pistols get my dick hard," Pop Somethin' laughed.

Queenie laughed with him. "Damn, Pop. What we gon' do?"

"Chase this mil, baby. And if anybody get in our way, we gon' push they shit back."

***

C-Note sat in the VIP section, staring out over the strip club. He was at Bonita's, a Latin strip club he had been frequenting as of late. It was a typical Friday night. Strippers walked around half-naked, shaking ass and picking up money. Normally C-Note's section would be filled with dancers and a good time would be had by all, but not today. The only person in the room this evening was Pop Somethin'.

"So, what's the move? Now that the feds up yo' ass, how much longer you finna do this shit?"

C-Note took a drink from the glass of Hennessey he had been nursing. "I gotta run it up until I get my day in court, bruh. I ain't got no choice. Feds is for real. I just wanna put shit in order before I go in."

"That's what I figured. So, what you want me to do? You know I expected shit to be different. I didn't make too many plans 'cause I was all in wit' chu. But now you in a jam."

"Just fuck wit' me 'til I go in. Ain't shit changed. Whatever you need, you got it."

"I'm makin' my own plans. I need to make my money grow fast. I wanna check a mil and move to Jamaica."

"What? Jamaica?"

"Yeah. Me and Queenie was talkin' the other night, and I wanna go back home and open up a hotel."

"You Jamaican? Where yo' accent at, nigga?"

"I don't got one. I been in Texas since I was six."

"Okay. I hear you, bruh. A mil, huh? You know I ain't seein' it like that, right? I just took a hundred thou hit."

"I know, but I got a li'l stash. I don't know too much about the hustle game, but if you finna stay in the game, I wanna invest in you. I got a hunnit Gs. What kinda return can I get of that?"

C-Note smiled. "Look at chu, nigga, soundin' like a businessman," he laughed. "But seriously, bruh, a hustla only as good as his connect. Big Poppi ain't gon' fuck wit' me now I'm fightin' this fed case. I need a new plug, and ABLE Team ain't fuckin' wit' us, either. They some bitches. Our only other option is right there."

Ray Gonzales, AKA Gonzo, was the second biggest cocaine distributer in Texas. The Mexican was short and stocky, face clean shaven except for a big-ass mustache. He didn't wear gaudy jewelry like most American drug dealers. He stayed true to his Mexican roots: a sombrero, an expensive dress shirt, fitted jeans, and a pair of hand-sown boots. He was sitting at a table in the middle of the club. Surrounding him and his men were twelve dancers. Stacks of money sat on the table, and the women were hanging around like vultures, trying to get some of the cash. At different spots in the club were Gonzo's security. They moved like the Secret Service, watching everything and everyone.

"Who is he?" Pop asked.

"Gonzo. Nigga like a God to Mexicans. They say he got dope by the tons from Mexico. His plug was El Chapo."

Pop's eyes bugged. "You bullshittin'?"

"Nah. That's what the streets say. If we can find a way to plug wit' him, shit, I won't even turn myself into the feds. I'll move to Mexico."

"But if he plugged wit' El Chapo, he won't fuck wit' us. Our money ain't long enough. A hunnit Gs ain't shit to him. Only way to plug wit' a nigga like him is if somebody vouch for us."

"I know, but it's a way in, though. I been watchin' this nigga for a couple weeks. He come here all the time. The bitch on his lap and the one behind him is his main freaks."

Pop Somethin' eyed the strippers. They looked good enough to be in movies. "Yeah. They bad."

"They also about to set him up."

Pop cut his eyes at C-Note. "What the fuck you talkin' 'bout?"

"Gonzo had most of these hos' family killed. Happened, like, twenty years ago. He don't even know who they is. He also left they brotha alive, Demon. He right there, by the bar."

A tall, skinny Mexican stood by the bar, sipping a drink and inconspicuously watching Gonzo. Most of the people in the club watched the baller, but the way Demon watched him was different. He had an issue.

"How the fuck you know all this shit?" Pop asked.

"I did my homework. I think it's goin' down when Gonzo an' 'em get in the parking lot. They can't do shit in this club because of the camera and security. Plus, Gonzo got bulletproof cars. They gotta get to him before he get to the cars in the lot. I think it's goin' down tonight."

Pop studied C-Note's face as all the information settled in his mind. "What the fuck you trynna get me in?"

"We in the right place at the right time. We keep our heads down 'til the hit, then we help Gonzo get them niggas off his ass."

"Look at chu, playin' chess wit' niggas' lives," Pop laughed. "That's a good move. But I got a better one. Let's dip to the parking lot right now and wait for the hit. Gonzo got trained security. Demon and his niggas is probably amateurs. They gon' die. We gotta come from behind and help them get Gonzo security outta the way. Then, right before they get to Gonzo, turn around and dump on Demon and his niggas."

A smile as big as the sun spread across C-Note's face. "Damn, nigga. If you'da signed up for the army, you coulda been a war general."

***

The parking lot was covered in darkness. Clouds blocked out the moon and stars, making the already black night seem even blacker. The only light that shown came from the club's neon sign above the entrance. A flash of

A GANGSTER'S CODE

light and the bass-pounding sound of Latin music filled the lot as Demon walked out of the club, followed by his three friends. They stopped at a caravan, popping the side door. Automatic rifles were passed around. After exchanging a few words, they took up positions. Demon was on the side of the building while his friends ducked behind cars in the parking lot.

A few minutes later another flash of light and more music filled the lot as the club door opened again. A four-man security detail scanned the lot like trained sentinels. When the squad leader gave the all-clear, two men went for the cars. Another went to grab the boss. It didn't take long for the door to open again. Two more security members stepped out of the club, followed by a large party of men and women. In the midst of the pack was Gonzo. He slapped asses and grabbed flesh, ready to finish the party at his estate.

When the kingpin was fully in view, Demon pointed the high powered rifle and squeezed the trigger.

Takka-takka-takka-takka-takka-takka-takka-takka-takka!

The parking lot was illuminated by flashes of light as automatic gunfire tore through the night. Screams filled the air as bullets pierced flesh. Two members of Gonzo's security team and three strippers lay on the ground bleeding. The other security members covered Gonzo and took cover behind a car parked near the entrance, then their battle training took over. The security team used hand signals to identify the shooters' positions. The two guards that had gone for the cars spotted Demon's shooters who were spread out in the parking lot. Shots to the head silenced the ambushers' automatic rifles.

The security was checking the bodies to make sure they were dead when the second ambush came. The .45 caliber bullets from Pop Somethin's Mac 12 chopped them down quickly, their blood mixing with the blood of their enemies. Pop Somethin' was on the move before their bodies stopped twitching, C-Note close behind.

The final battle scene showed Demon in a firefight with the last two security members. They had him surrounded and were seconds away from the kill. Nobody noticed Pop Somethin' and C-Note coming from behind.

Pop-pop-pop-pop-pop-pop-pop-pop!
Fwop-fwop-fwop-fwop-fwop!

C-Note and Pop Somethin' took the security down quickly. Demon brought his head out from hiding, thinking his boys had come to his rescue. When he seen the infrared dot from C-Note's Glock shine in his eyes, he knew his time was up. The bullet went through his right eye and out the back of his head.

They found Gonzo huddled behind a car with the two strippers who had set him up. "You a'ight?" C-Note asked.

When the godfather looked up and seen the guns in C-Note and Pop Somethin's hands, he got hostile. "What do you want? Do you know who I am?"

Pop Somethin' spoke up. "I think you got it mixed up, big man. We just saved yo' ass. You can roll wit' us or stay here 'til the police come."

"No! Where are my guards? Juanito? Jorge!" he called.

"They all dead, man. This yo' last chance, or we leavin' without you."

Gonzo stood up and looked around. Dead bodies were strewn out all over the parking lot. After one more look at

A GANGSTER'S CODE

C-Note and Pop Somethin', he nodded. "Okay. I'm ready. Let's go."

"What about them?" Pop asked, looking at the strippers.

"No witnesses."

Gonzo looked sad. "I understand. No witnesses."

Terrified looks spread across the women's faces right before Pop Somethin' shot them in their heads.

***

"Who were they?" Gonzo asked, moving around uncomfortably in the backseat of the Infinity.

"I dunno. I know we came to see some ass and heard the shots," Pop Somethin' answered.

"Who are you? Why did you help?"

"I'm C-Note. This my nigga, Pop Somethin'. Everybody in Texas know who you is, Gonzo. Shit, you a legend. We couldn't let them fuck-niggas take you out. The streets need you, my nigga."

"You fools, but I thank you for foolishness. I admit I never much cared for blacks, but you two have opened my ignorant mind. *Muchas gracias.*"

"No problem, boss. But you kept it a li'l too real on that black shit. But I hear you," C-Note said.

"Sorry, *mi amigo*. I am blunt speaker. I mean no disrespect. Do you have phone? I need to make call."

C-Note passed his phone to Gonzo and listened intently, trying to decipher the Mexican's Spanish. The boss cursed and yelled and cursed throughout the call, and C-Note didn't understand a single word.

"Drive me to meet my people. I appreciate it. What you did must be rewarded. If I can do anything for you, let me know and it will be done."

Chapter 11

One month later

The opening of Lux was an event. With the knowledge gained from throwing concerts, C-Note's marketing skills put the opening of his strip club over the top. Radio advertisement, print ads, social media, and word of mouth had everybody who was somebody and a bunch of nobodies at the grand opening. What separated Lux from other strip clubs in Dallas was the ocean theme. Giant twenty-foot long fish tanks were spread throughout the club. Inside them were all kinds of marine life: octopuses, squids, eels, turtles, and all kinds of fish. The most impressive tank was in the middle of the club. The four-foot tall, one-hundred square foot tank was the main stage. Inside the tank were baby sharks.

"C-Note, you outdid yo'self wit' dis one, boy. Damn! I ain't neva seen nuttin' like dis, man. Dem real octopuses?" a club-goer asked, looking around like he was standing in the Taj Mahal.

"C'mon, bruh. You know I don't do nothin' halfway. Wait 'til you see the main show on the shark stage. Ain't nobody neva did it like me. Lux goin' down in history!"

"Yeah, mans. You definitely doin' it! Now all you gotta do is get one of yo' girls to gimme a free lap dance. Dey walkin' 'round here lookin' like mermaids. Make a nigga wanna take a swim," he laughed.

"C'mon, bruh. It don't cost nothin' to look, but chu gotta pay to touch."

"I'm fuckin' wit' chu, C-Note. But I love yo' spot. You 'bout to shut down all the clubs in Dallas. They gon' have to step they game up. A'ight, man. Lemme get back to watchin' all this ass."

C-Note smiled as he watched the stranger walk away. Everyone was having a good time, laughing, drinking, dancing, spending money. Niggas was already making it rain, and the main show hadn't even started yet.

C-Note was about to go find Artie and Lucci when a tall Mexican walked into the club. He wore a dark, tailored suit and a serious face. "Damn, Edwardo, smile sometimes. Where the big man at? I been waitin' on him all night."

The security guard looked around the club suspiciously as he spoke. "He outside. I came to take a look around, see where our party will be."

"I got y'all in VIP, especially built for high-profile people. Got a view of both exits and the main stage. I even picked a couple Latin girls to keep him company. Go get the boss. I need him to celebrate wit' me."

After a last look around, Edwardo left. He came back a couple minutes later with a party of eight: five bodyguards, Gonzo, and two men C-Note had never seen before. Security took Gonzo and his people directly to the VIP section.

Club Lux had ten of them. They weren't rooms, but spacious coves in the walls. They were separated from the club by Plexiglas windows that, at the push of a button, would change from transparent to snow white. This gave the guests privacy. Inside each cove were couches, tables, and a stripper pole.

After Gonzo was settled in, C-Note went to pay a visit. "Gonzo! What up, big man?"

"C-Note! How are you, *mi amigo*? I see the grand opening is good, no?"

A GANGSTER'S CODE

"It's better than good. It's great! You see, all these people came to be part of the new era in strip clubs."

"And what do they think about the upgrades? Nobody has fish tanks and sharks. This makes you one-of-a-kind, no?"

"At first I thought you was trippin' when you told me about the tanks, but after seein' the blueprints and now the finished project, you a genius, man. That's why you the boss of all bosses. And it don't hurt that yo' investment helped pay for it all. I couldn't've did this without you."

"You are too, kind, my friend. Too kind. I cannot thank you enough for saving my life. What I've done for you is a small thing. Money is nothing. Loyalty cannot be bought. Oh, and these are my son and nephew, Omar and Julio. They have secret thing for dark skin, so I bring them," he laughed.

"It's all good. Ain't nothin' in the world taste better than chocolate. Hey, I gotta get out on this floor and mingle some more. I'ma send you some bottle girls and dancers. Let me know if y'all need anything."

"Okay, *mi amigo*. Send the best girls. I feel good tonight. And where is Shooter?"

"He out here movin' around. I'ma let him know you here when I see him."

After leaving the VIP section, c-Note went to find Pop Somethin'. He was by the bar wearing a serious face, watching the crowd.

"Damn, nigga. Do you eva just chill and have a good time? Why you always serious?'"

"What chu think I'm doin', nigga?" Pop said, taking a sip from his drink.

"This not havin' fun, bruh. Go get some lap dances. Make it rain. Party. Turn up."

"My bitch a stripper. I can get a lap dance whenever I want. I ain't one of these stupid-ass niggas that check a bag just to throw it in the air or give it to some bitches I ain't finna fuck. Niggas is stupid. You don't gotta throw money to have a good time, and turnin' up is how niggas slip and get killed. I'm cool wit' my cranberry on ice and watchin' niggas act stupid."

C-Note shook his head at Pop before turning to the bartender. "Kesha, send some girls to the VIP to check on my boy Gonzo, and let me get a bottle of Cîroc. This nigga blowin' my buzz."

"How long Gonzo been here?" Pop asked.

"I don't know, not that long. He asked about you."

"I'ma make my way to see him in a minute. You still ain't gon' tell him 'bout the fed case? You know if he find out, shit gon' get sour."

"C'mon, Pop. You know I can't do that. He the best plug I ever had. Whole thang fo' five Gs. And he dropped a hundred on them fish tanks just to say thanks for savin' his life. Shit, I'ma run it up for as long as I can. When he find out, I'ma let him cut the ties. By then you should have yo' mil and I should be set. Shit, we both should be millionaires real soon."

"That's a fucked up plan, C-Note. He a cartel boss. You think he gon' let chu walk away? Gonzo and the niggas he fuck wit' play for keeps. One way in, one way out."

"I don't got no choice. I'm burnin' up either way it go. I'd rather keep doin' what I'm doin' than break it off. I ain't neva had it like this, and this money too sweet to walk away. I gotta ride this out and see where it go."

Pop gave him a long stare. "A'ight. It's yo' life."

"Fuck that shit. Where Queenie an' 'em at? It's 'bout time for the show to start."

"I just seen 'em. They in the back."

"I'ma go check on 'em. Go holla at Gonzo."

C-Note spun away from Pop Somethin', about to head to the back room when something caught his eye. No, not something. Someone. Franco. Him and ABLE Team had just walked in. They were ten deep, men and women. They all wore surprise and awe on their faces as they looked around. C-Note forgot about Queenie as he went to greet ABLE Team. This was his opportunity to jack and stunts. He wanted to humiliate Franco like he had been humiliated when he first got out of prison.

"Franco, what's good? I see ABLE Team in the buildin'!" C-Note smiled.

"So, this you, huh? For real, for real?" Franco asked, an envious look in his eyes.

"Yeah. I told you I was gon' do it big. This that lucrative shit I was tellin' you 'bout. You see my nigga Gonzo in VIP," C-Note pointed out. "I fuck wit' bosses. Hunnit Gs on fish tanks an' shit. I know most niggas ain't gotta hunnit racks to spend on fish. Nigga, my main stage is a shark tank! Real sharks, nigga!" C-Note laughed.

Franco and the rest of ABLE Team mugged C-Note, but he didn't care. He was feeling himself.

"Yeah, you doin' it, bruh. I didn't see this comin'," Franco said, sucking the back of his teeth.

"I know. Most niggas can't look at a tree and see a house. You gotta have vision for that," C-Note laughed, loving the look on Franco's face as he gave him a dose of his own medicine. "Lemme getcha all a spot in the VIP. I know you didn't ask for it, but it's on me. Show you how we do it in the Lux."

C-Note led ABLE Team to a VIP cove, standing at the door as they passed by. And that's when he noticed the two women. It was Franco's wife and her sister. Michelle noticed C-Note at the same time he noticed her. Her eyes grew wide as the moon when recognition set in. Pop Somethin's warning about leaving witnesses flashed in C-Note's mind.

He turned his head, trying to avoid her, but he knew it was too late.

"A'ight, y'all. Chill and relax. I'ma send some bottle girls," C-Note said before leaving. Panic rushed through him as he left the cove. Of all the nights for him to run into Franco's girl, it had to be the night of the grand opening of Lux. He tried to process the possible outcomes, but kept coming up with one: a shootout with Radar in the middle of the club. That would ruin his opening, and possibly his success. He needed to find Pop Somethin' and come up with a plan. His success depended on it.

Fortunately the shooter wasn't far. The muscle-bound, bearded killer stuck out in the club like a white girl at the Million Man March. He was in the VIP cove with Gonzo. C-Note rushed into the room like he had fire ants in his pants. "Pop, lemme holla at chu!"

Everyone in the room could hear the panic in his voice. Gonzo spoke up. "You okay, *amigo*?"

C-Note gave a fake smile. "Yeah. Uh, I just. It's just some business. I need to borrow Shooter."

Pop Somethin' eyed C-Note as they left the VIP cove and walked through the club. "Fuck wrong wit' chu, nigga?"

A GANGSTER'S CODE

"It's all bad, Pop. Let's go toward the back. Look in VIP cove six."

Pop Somethin' searched until he found what C-Note was talking about. His eyes immediately locked with Franco, and then Radar. They stood with aggressive looks on their faces, watching C-Note and Pop Somethin'. "I see yo' girlfriends showed up," Pop laughed.

"They know I robbed 'em. He brought his girl and her sister. Soon as she seen me, she got spooked. Damn, I shoulda wore a mask. These niggas gon' fuck up my grand openin'. Fuck!"

"I don't wanna say I told you so, but I told you so. Neva leave a witness, my nigga. Mommas, daddies, aunties. E'erybody gotta go. Even kids, 'cause they can grow up and fuck you up when they get old enough. But you should be good for now. It's cameras in here, so they shouldn't do shit. Where Artie an' 'em?"

"They runnin' 'round here somewhere. Fuck! If this nigga fuck up my opening, I'm killin' they whole family. Kids and all. E'erybody gotta go!"

Pop laughed. "Chill out, nigga. Tell Artie and Lucci to lay low and out the way. Ain't no sense in them niggas gettin' in this shit, even though Franco prolly know they was wit' chu. If you want, we can grab Beast Mode and Trench and put they ass out. That way we don't give 'em a chance to do shit in the club."

C-Note turned up. "Hell yeah! Get they bitch-asses outta here! I can't risk them fuckin' up my spot or shootin' one of my tanks. Put 'em out!"

Pop Somethin' grabbed four security guards, including Beast Mode and Trench. All of them were big and muscular. They moved toward VIP cove six like men on mission.

Pop was the first person in the room. "I hate to break up y'all party, but y'all gotta go!"

Radar jumped to his feet, hand close to his waist.

"If you pull it, you betta use it," Pop warned.

The shooters had a stare-down. Hostilities were exchanged without them saying a word.'

"Chill, Radar," Franco spoke up, standing to his feet. "So, this how it is, C-Note? You gon' get cho goons to kick me out cho club? My money ain't no good?"

"It ain't like that. This a business decision. I gotta do what's best for my business."

Franco turned up. "My money started this business, nigga! Yo' coward-ass robbed my bitch while I was outta town, fuck-nigga! Put my nephew in a coma. I'ma leave yo' bitch-ass club. Too many witnesses. But don't think this shit clever, nigga. You gon' get yours!"

C-Note wasn't about to let Franco get the last word, so he turned it up a notch. "Fuck you, yo' bitch, and yo' nephew, nigga. I shoulda cooked his li'l ho-ass!"

Franco made a move like he was goin' for C-Note. A security guard grabbed the ABLE Team leader. Radar went to protect his boss and punched the security guard in the face. Pop Somethin' swung on Radar, sending ABLE Team's shooter stumbling backward toward the couch. After he caught his balance, Radar went for his waist.

Pop Somethin' was faster. Before Radar could pull his pistol, Pop had a Glock pointed in his face. "You 'bout to piss me off! Move yo' hand or I'ma knock yo' shit back," Pop threatened.

Radar moved slowly, mugging Pop Somethin' as he lowered his hand. With all the ass and action happening in the club, only a few people noticed the commotion in the VIP area.

A GANGSTER'S CODE

After taking the clip from Radar's gun, the security squad kicked ABLE Team out of the club. "You know that just started some shit, right?" Pop Somethin' told C-Note.

"I know. Damn. As soon as shit start lookin' up for me, I gotta get drug back in the gutta."

"That's life, my nigga. Ups and downs. Hills and valleys. Bitter and sweet. It's all about how you react to what life throw at chu. We know what's comin'. You wanna play offense or defense?"

"Damn, Pop. I don't wanna focus on this shit right now. I just wanna deal with tonight. I need everybody to have a good time. I need to put Lux on the map."

"A'ight. You handle the business. I'ma handle security. It's 'bout time for the main show. Go handle that."

***

The lights in the club dimmed as Blac Youngsta's *Booty* flowed through Lux's state-of-the-art sound system. The main stage was dark. Even the lights in the tank were off, but slowly they came on, revealing the baby sharks swimming frantically in a panicked state. Two big, shiny, fish-like creatures swam from the back of the tank. At first glance they looked like adult sharks swimming with the babies.

Upon further inspection, they weren't sharks, but humans. Women painted in silver body paint with mermaid fins on their feet. They wore goggles, breathing masks, and small oxygen tanks on their backs. They swam up to the front of the tank, pressing their flesh against the glass and doing water tricks. The women in the water looked identical. It was Queenie and her sister Princess. After entertaining the crowd with seductive aquatic techniques, they swam to the back of the tank, disappearing from sight.

Movement on the stage got everyone's attention. A tall, thick woman with fiery-red hair crab-walked into view. It was Skittlez. Her face and hands were painted red, and she wore a red body suit. The latex fit her body like a glove, showing off her killer curves. She danced around the stage, shaking her ass and gyrating to the music. Then she moved to the pole and did tricks, twists, and turns most women in pole dancing classes were afraid to try.

And just when the crowd thought the main event couldn't get any better, it did. Queenie and Princess came from behind the curtain crawling on their knees. The twins had shed their mermaid gear and were naked except for the silver body paint and silver thongs. Although they were twins, they didn't have the same body structure. Queenie was thick and curvy. Princess was slim with an athletic build. While Skittlez worked the pole, the twins worked the stage. They tumbled, twerked, did the splits, grinded on each other, and slapped ass.

When Skittlez joined them, the stage heated up. The red-painted stripper went over to Queenie and kissed her aggressively. Princess got in on the kissing right before the sisters began pawing at the body-hugging latex suit, ripping holes and exposing Skittlez's red-painted flesh. They continued ripping her suit until she was naked, then they ripped each other's thongs off.

When everybody was butt-naked, the freak show began. A pussy-licking threesome brought money raining down on the stage. Skittlez was on her back, Queenie was between her legs, and Princess rode the red-painted woman's face. Silver and red bodies gyrated in sexual rhythms. Then Princess stood to her feet, fingering her clit above Skittlez's face. At that same instant Queenie's pussy-eating skills had Skittlez's orgasm building. The redhead arched her back and let out a scream of passion. The sound of Skittlez passion pushed Princess over the edge. She lifted her head toward the ceiling and cried out as clear fluid gushed from her pussy onto Skittlez's face.

    C-Note stood by the stage, clapping with the rest of the crowd. He knew the performance had entertained the crowd and everybody would be talking about his club. Lux would be the best thing smoking in Dallas for a long time.

J-BLUNT

Chapter 12

"Queenie, wake up! Queenie," Princess called, shaking her sister awake.

"What, Princess? Damn! I'm trynna sleep," she said groggily. They had another late night at Lux and she was dead tired.

"It's almost noon. Get up. I need you to show me around. I ran outta pills. Where the percs at, bitch?"

"Tell Pop. I'm sleep."

"Pop gone. Get up."

Queenie perked up and looked around the room. When she confirmed Pop was really gone, she looked at her sister. They shared the same dark chocolate skin, chinky eyes, and high cheekbones. Their hair was also dreadlocked with reddish-blonde dye. The only way to tell them apart was the silver studs in Princess' cheeks and their body shapes. The slimmer sister stood at the foot of the bed wearing a body-hugging yellow jumpsuit and black knee-high leather boots.

"Yo' ass woke up when you heard yo' man was gone. Don't tell me you fallin' in love. You know how we do."

Queenie rolled her eyes. "Shut up, bitch. It ain't like that."

"What is it like, then? You the one talkin' 'bout movin' to Jamaica wit' this nigga. You only knew him a couple months. You movin' way too fast."

"I know it seem fast, but Pop is different. He not like other niggas I fucked wit'. He real."

"You said the same thing about Travis back in the day. That nigga didn't think twice about givin' me some dick."

"Gurl, we was sixteen. I didn't know no better. Travis was a forty-year-old pedophile fuckin' wit' us. And you wasn't supposed to fuck him. It was a test to see if he would. Key word 'would.'"

"Well, he did. And he wasn't shit. Just like Chauncey. Niggas ain't shit. It's s'posed to be me and you. We fuck these niggas and get money. What about that?"

Queenie rolled her eyes again and sucked her teeth.

Princess got an attitude. "Don't roll yo' eyes at me, bitch! What about us? It's me and you, right?"

"C'mon, sis. You already know that. But Pop Somethin' is a good nigga. And he not like them otha niggas. We made plans to get out this shit and make a better life in Jamaica. We can't rob and fuck niggas forever. We already burnt up H-Town. We gotta think about the future. We gotta think past the next check."

Princess stared at her sister like she was from another planet. "Bitch, I don't even know you right now. How you sound? We just ran up a check at Lux. Twenty-five thou in three nights. Dallas is alive. All this million-dollar, hotel shit ain't real. That's Pop dream. We gotta live real life. Plus, he might not be around much longer. Drama and Snot lookin' for y'all."

Queenie sat up. "What they say?"

"You know they not finna let him get away wit' killin' Yea. Pop Squad don't play that shit. That's why you need to get away from this nigga. He got enemies all over Texas."

"What about Deso? He lookin' for us, too?"

"Nah. Deso worship Pop Somethin'. He told Drama and Snot to leave y'all alone. They damn near fought over that shit, but we family, so they figured it out. Deso know how they feel, but he not gettin' involved."

A GANGSTER'S CODE

"What about you? You gon' tell them where we live?"

Princess's demeanor softened as she walked over and sat on the bed. When the sisters were face-to-face, Princess reached out and ran her hand through Queenie's dreads. "You know where my loyalty at. It's with you. I'm not gon' let Pop Somethin' or Pop Squad come between us. I love you, sis, and I'm not gon' do nothin' to hurt you. I know you feelin' Pop Somethin', and because yo' feelin's in it, I ain't tellin' Pop Squad shit."

Queenie smiled lovingly at her sister, leaning in for a kiss. After a peck on the lips, Princess stood to her feet. "Now, get up, bitch. I need some beans. And later we finna find Skittlez's good pussy-ass. I wanna fuck her again."

***

Pop Somethin' grabbed a stack of bills from the table and stuffed it into the duffel bag. The money stack held five thousand dollars. He put ten stacks in the bag before zipping it closed. After putting the bag on the floor, he looked up at the crisscrossing machetes that hung on the wall. He was sitting on the couch in C-Note's playa pad. This was where he took females to fuck or had meetings with people he didn't want to bring to his house. The crib was plush and had all the latest tech gadgets. The crisscrossing machetes always caught Pop's eye. His father walked around with a machete, and seeing the blade reminded him of home.

"Where you get them from?" Pop asked.

C-Note looked up from counting money to see what Pop was talking about. "Somebody was about to throw 'em away. I took 'em and hung 'em up. Shit remind me of some African tribal shit. Zulu warriors, nigga," he laughed.

"So, you slept here again? Carla still at cho house?" Pop asked, noticing C-Note was wearing a t-shirt and jogging pants.

"I love my sister, bruh, but I can't wait 'til she get the fuck outta, my house. I'm to the point where I'm thinkin' 'bout movin' in here. I can't do all those kids-n-shit. I love my nephews, but they too much."

"Why you just don't get her a house? You can stand it."

"'Cause I always gave her everything. She don't know the meaning of working hard and gettin' her own shit, so I stopped. She gotta be independent and quit dependin' on me or a nigga."

"She yo' big sister, bruh. And she thirty years old. If she ain't figured it out now, she prolly won't."

"All I know is I ain't givin' her shit. She gon' save them checks and get her own shit."

"Or just stay where she at and take over yo' shit," Pop laughed.

"Fuck you, dawg!" C-Note said, throwing a stack of money at Pop Somethin'.

"So, what chu wanna do about ABLE Team? We really don't got enough niggas to start a war. Artie and Lucci yo' niggas, but they soft."

"I know. Them niggas ain't no shooters, but ABLE Team ain't really what niggas think they is. If we get Franco and Radar out the way, the rest of them niggas gon' fold."

"That's what you wanna do?" Pop asked.

"Not really. This money good, and I don't wanna start no war. Lux is poppin'. Artie and Lucci runnin' it up on the highway. A war gon' fuck shit up."

"You watch sports?"

C-Note frowned. "What kinda question is that? We talkin' 'bout war, nigga."

"A good offense gon' beat a good defense all day. You know Franco an' 'em gon' eventually come, and it's more of them than us."

"Yeah, I know. But right now I need you to help me play defense. When the time is right, we gon' play offense."

Pop gave him a long stare. "A'ight, I'm wit' chu, my nigga. I like some of the security at Lux. Beast Mode and Trench certified. I'ma strap some of them niggas up."

"Yeah, that's what I'm talkin' 'bout. Be my war general."

***

Pop noticed Queenie's Nissan Maxima was gone as he pulled the Infinity into the driveway. After grabbing the duffle bag from the backseat, he went in the house. The first thing he noticed was the alarm wasn't set. He made a mental note to get at Queenie about that.

After locking the door, he headed for the basement. The lower level had been converted into an entertainment room. A 70-inch TV hung on the wall with all kinds of electronics hooked up to it. Four recliner chairs sat in front of the TV. Behind the entertainment area was a small bar. There were two rooms on the right wall, one of them a workout room, the other a laundry room. That's where he went. Inside was a washer, dryer, and folding table. What couldn't be seen was the removable section of the south wall. Pop pushed in a panel and the wall opened, revealing shelves lined with guns, ammo, and body armor. An AR-15, M-16, Mini-14, and automatic 12-gauge made up the heavy artillery. Two Taurus 9mms, two Sig Sauer 357s, two Glock 40s, and a Mac-11 made up the small arms. There were also three lightweight Kevlar vests. Below the guns was a safe. He put in the combo. Inside was one-hundred thousand dollars in neat stacks. After adding the fifty thousand he got from C-Note, he stared at the money. He was well on his way to a mil. If things kept moving the way they were, he would reach his goal by the end of the year.

A noise from upstairs forced him to forget about his million-dollar plans. Somebody was in his house. After closing the safe, he pulled a .45 from his shoulder holster and crept up the stairs. The noise had come from the living room. On the way through the kitchen, he peeked out the window to see if Queenie had come home. The only vehicle in the driveway was his truck. He moved quietly through the kitchen, pausing at the threshold of the living room. He peeked around the corner and seen a female kneeling on the floor, her ass in the air. When he seen the reddish-blonde dreadlocks, he relaxed.

"Where yo' car, Queenie? I thought you was gone."

Princess jumped and spun around quickly. "Oh, shit! Don't be creepin' up on me like that! Make some noise or somethin'. What you got the gun for?"

"My bad. I heard some noise and thought somebody was breakin' in. Then I thought you was Queenie. Y'all look just alike. Where she at?" he asked, holstering the gun.

A GANGSTER'S CODE

"I don't know. Her and Skittlez out bein' hos. I dropped my jambalaya on the floor. Shit was good, too," she said before going back to picking up the food.

"I'ma let you get back to that," Pop said, heading for the basement.

"Wait, wait, wait! Talk to me for a minute."

Pop leaned against the wall, looking Princess over from head to toe, judging her intent. He hadn't talked to her much since she had come to town, but her facial expression showed curiosity and mischief. "What you wanna talk about?"

Princess walked past, brushing her ass against his arm as she walked into the kitchen. "You and my sister," she said, throwing away the food and washing her hands.

"What you wanna know?"

She took her time responding, wiping her hands and spinning to face him. "You and my sister seem serious."

"What she say?"

"That y'all movin' to Jamaica. That sound serious."

"That's the plan. You got a problem with that?"

"Yeah. She my twin. We do everything together. We had our own plans. Now that she met you, she changed 'em."

"Don't you want what's best for her? What y'all doin' wit' Pop Squad ain't gon' last. Y'all already burnt up Houston. Y'all been jackin' for years and ain't got shit to show for it. Blowin' money fast not worth a grave or cell. You see, what we doin' in Dallas, we got a goal."

Princess leaned against the sink and cut her eyes at Pop Somethin'. "But what about her heart?"

"What about it?"

"Queenie is submissive and a li'l mushy. She don't got the stomach to hang wit' chu. She got dreams of fallin' in love and gettin' married. That shit ain't real, especially wit' a nigga like you. I heard all the people you shot and killed. Queenie not cut out for that shit."

"Yo' first mistake was thinkin' you know me. Second was you thinkin' you know Queenie. Yeah, she submissive because she know her place. She my bitch. That don't make her weak. She understand boundaries and roles. For any relationship to work, you gotta have understandin'. We got that. And you need to ask yo' sister 'bout her stomach. You'd be surprised how strong she is."

"Oh, okay," she nodded, understanding why Queenie was so taken with Pop. Not only was he a physical beast, but he was a thinker. "I got you now. Did you promise to marry her and give her all those damn kids she want?"

"Nah. I'm real. I don't sell dreams or tell lies. I didn't tell Queenie I was gon' marry her or that I love her. That shit ain't for us. What we got his based on loyalty, not love. She my bitch. I'm her nigga. Ride or die."

The kitchen was silent as the two had a stare-down. Pop figured out Princes was the dominant sister with a dominant personality. She led. Queenie followed. Princess was also manipulative. He could see her twisting niggas and bitches around her finger, bending them to her will. At that moment he realized Queenie and Princess were a package deal. If he wanted to keep Queenie in line and focused on the mission, he would have to bring Princess along, too. And that wouldn't be easy.

"Where yo' loyalty at?" he asked.

"Wit' my sister."

"What about Pop Squad?"

"Wit' them, too. To a certain degree."

"What degree is that? Either you loyal or you not."

"It ain't that easy. Them my niggas. I fucks wit' them, but I'm not gon' do nothin' to hurt me or Queenie. If it comes down to us or them, it's gon' be them."

"Loyalty is a sacrifice. Openin' yo'self up to hurt, harm, and danger for the benefit of whoever you loyal to. You ain't loyal to Pop Squad at all. Them niggas a meal, just like the tricks you fuck wit', otherwise you woulda told them where I live by now. I see you, Princess. *Namaste*."

She frowned. "What the fuck you just say?"

"*Namaste*. The Indians say that. It means 'I bow to the inner you', but I loosely translate it in this instance to mean I see you for who you really are."

She waved off his words. "Nigga, you just met me. You don't know me. Everything you say sound slick, but I ain't Queenie."

"I know, 'cause Queenie woulda already been on her knees suckin' my dick."

"Don't talk about my sister like that!" she flared up.

He challenged her. "Why? Cause I'm tellin' the truth?"

"Nah, because you takin' advantage of her."

"Like you. You took advantage of her all y'all life. Told her what to do and who to be. What if you wrong about me and I'm the one lettin' her be who she really is?"

Princess looked like she wanted to hurt Pop. "Fuck you, nigga. You don't know me."

"You already told me that."

Princess couldn't hide her ire. Her eyes were angry slits, her nostrils flared, and her top lip quivered. She wanted to attack him. Hurt him. Break him down to size like she did most people who challenged her. But she knew this was a fight she couldn't win, so she walked away.

Pop smiled when she walked by him. He had gotten under her skin, exactly what he wanted to do. Now she knew he wasn't the average nigga. He wasn't just a physical force, but a mental one, as well.

For the next part of his plan, he needed Queenie's approval. He pulled out his phone and sent her a text. She called him back, Facetiming.

"Hey, baby. Everything okay?"

"Me and Princess need to get an understandin'."

Confusion spread across Queenie's face. "What happened?"

"I'ma give you the details later. You trust me?"

"You know I do, Pop. You my nigga."

"So, no matter what happens between me and her, you still gon' be my bitch?"

The confused look on Queenie's face turned to worry. "Don't hurt my sister. Please."

"You out wit' Skittlez, right?"

"Yeah, but I can come –"

"Nah, don't come home. Find somethin' to do. I see her for who she is. She yo' protector. I know I can't have you without her. I'm finna go get her."

The worry vanished from Queenie's face as a smile spread across her lips. "Get her, baby."

***

Pop found Princess in his bedroom, sitting on the bed, her face in her phone. He stopped in the doorway and watched her.

When she felt his presence, she looked up, mugging him. "I don't feel like talkin' no more shit. Stay outta my way and I'ma stay outta yours."

Pop stepped into the room and dropped his gun holsters on the floor. "I got a proposition for you."

She took a deep breath, exhaling loudly. "What, nigga? What?"

Even though she was hostile, Pop remained calm. "Don't go back to Houston. Fuck Pop Squad. Them niggas gon' get you killed. I want you on my team. Be my bitch."

She laughed loudly, looking him from head to toe. "What the fuck kinda pills you takin'? Gimme some, 'cause these percs ain't got shit on what you be on."

"I don't take pills. You shouldn't either, and we gon' work on that. You see the kinda money you can make at Lux. Twenty-five racks in one weekend. You ain't neva did that in Houston. That happened because of me. I put Queenie in the right place, and you benefited from it. You already loyal to me because you loyal to Queenie. You my bitch and don't even know it. Stay and make it official."

Princess shook her head as she got up from the bed. "You way too much for me. I'm bookin' into a hotel. I'ma call a Uber and wait outside."

When she tried to walk past, Pop manhandled her, pushing her against the wall and throwing her phone across the room. Princess was surprised and intimidated by his strength, speed, and size. She was five-foot-four and he was six-foot-six. He towered over her like a giant, holding her against the wall by her arms.

"Let me go, Pop! Get off me!" she growled, struggling to free her arms.

His voice was forceful and calm at the same time. "Stop. Look at me."

Princess looked him in his eyes, holding his stare.

"I'm offerin' you life. A way out the bullshit. Security. Loyalty. Opportunity. Somethin' nobody never gave you. I told you I see you. I wasn't bullshittin'. You big sis. You take care of Queenie. But who take care of you? I can do that. You see me. You know I'm real. You just scared 'cause you ain't neva had this. You used to runnin' shit, and this seem too good. I'm tellin' you that yo' place is wit' me. I got you."

Princess stood before him like a child, staring up at him like he was the answer to all of her prayers. When he released her arms, she stood there, waiting for him to make the next move. He lowered his head to kiss her and Princess came to life, attacking his lips and tongue with aggressive kisses.

Pop reached behind her, fumbling with the zipper on the back of her jumper. When he couldn't unzip it, he grabbed two handfuls of the fabric and pulled. Princess moaned as the material was ripped from her back and shoulders. Then she went for his shirt, ripping strips of cotton, dropping them on the floor. She went for his pants next, unbuckling them and dropping them to his ankles. Then his boxers

Pop stepped out of his clothes and ripped off more of her jumpsuit. She wore no panties or bra underneath. When her lady parts were free, he lifted her like a ragdoll, his arms beneath her legs. Her arms folded behind his neck as she hung on. He held her against the wall and penetrated her deep until their pelvises were touching.

"Oh, shit!" she cursed, biting him on his bearded cheek and grabbing hold of his dreads.

A GANGSTER'S CODE

He started with slow, long strokes, holding her in place as he dug her guts out. Princess was on cloud nine as she cursed, bit, scratched, and pulled his dreads. The aggressive fuck session made Pop speed up. He rammed his dick in and out of her with fast, hard strokes.

"Oh, gawd! Oh, gawd! Oh, gawd!" Princess cried, lost in a zone between pain and ultimate pleasure. When she came, it felt like everything inside her dissolved and oozed out of her pussy. And it wasn't just one orgasm. They came in waves.

Pop Felt like he was on Viagra. His dick was super hard, and his stamina was amazing. He held her in the air, pounding her pussy for twenty minutes. Her juices dripped down his legs and onto the floor, pooling at his feet. When he felt his leg muscles tightening, he took her over to the bed and fell on top, continuing to pound out. When he finally busted his nut, he growled like a bear, filling her with his seed. They huffed and puffed like bulls, staring into each other's eyes, challenging one another silently. Pop knew he needed a moment. The tingling of his dick wouldn't allow him to move, so Princess took over, flipping him on his back and climbing on top.

"Awe, shit!" Pop grunted, gritting his teeth as he fought through the pleasure and pain shooting through his dick.

Princess didn't waste time getting into a rhythm. She grabbed two handfuls of his beard and rode him like jockey riding Sea Biscuit. The noises she made weren't all human. She growled, moaned, whimpered, screamed, and cried. The pulling of his beard hurt like nothing Pop had ever felt, but he soldiered on.

When she came, she lifted her head to the ceiling and screamed, pulling his beard so hard she pulled his mouth open, forcing him to scream with her. He could feel her cum pooling in his dick-hairs and dripping down his balls and ass crack. Princess shook and collapsed on top of him.

Pop didn't give her time to recuperate. He pushed her off him and onto her stomach, then he got behind her, grabbing her hips and pulling her onto her knees, doggy style.

"Oh, Pop! Shit, nigga! Damn!"

He pulled her dreads and slapped her ass while he fucked her. Princess came again. And again. And again. When she couldn't take no more, she fell onto her stomach, drained. Pop stayed on top of her, humping away.

"Okay, Pop! You win! You win!"

Her words were music to his ears. "Who's bitch is you?"

"Yours! Yours!"

"You my bitch, right? You my bitch?"

"Yeah, Pop! Yeah!"

Pop continued to beat it up, loving the power her words made him feel. "Say it. Tell me you my bitch."

"I'm yo' bitch, Pop! I'm yo' bitch!"

"Say 'fuck Pop Squad.'"

"Okay! Fuck Pop Squad! Fuck them niggas!"

Chapter 13

The silver Benz glided into the parking lot of Wells Fargo, parking next to a white Ford Explorer. C-Note pulled out his phone and sent a text. Less than a minute later, Shanice walked out wearing a purple, frilly blouse, tight white skirt, and purple heels. Her hair flowed past her shoulders in long curls, bouncing and swaying as she walked quickly to the Benz.

"Damn, gurl. e'ery time I see you, you get finer," C-Note complimented as she sat in the passenger seat.

"Awe, thanks," she blushed. "Now hurry up and pull outta here before one of my coworkers see us. I ain't trynna explain this to nobody or get judged."

"Chill, baby. You know I ain't gon' do nothin' to get us knocked. Let cho seat back and relax."

After hearing the comforting words, Shanice leaned over and kissed him before reclining in her seat. "So, what do you have planned that is so much a secret you can't tell me?"

"I'm not tellin' you. That's why it's called a secret. You'll see when we get there. You ever heard this song before? Every time I hear it, I think of you." When he turned up the radio, Dej Loaf and Jacquees' *In The Club* filled the car.

"This my song!" Shanice sang, snapping her fingers.

Five minutes later they parked in front of a photography studio called Beautiful Images. Shanice looked surprised. "What is this?"

"A photography studio. I'ma explain why we here in a second, but it's somethin' I need to tell you."

The seriousness in his tone made Shanice curl her face. "What's goin' on, baby? I don't like the way you sound."

He took a deep breath. "I got jammed by the twelve a couple months ago. The feds. My lawyers say they gon' draw the case out for as long as they can, but I'm prolly not gon' beat it."

Shanice looked like she had been punched in the stomach. Her eyes popped, jaw dropped, and she was speechless.

"Say somethin', Shanice. You a'ight?"

When she found her voice, the questions rushed out like a run-on sentence. "What did you do? You gotta go to jail? For how long?"

"They caught me wit' twenty birds."

Her eyes threatened to pop out of her head. "Twenty kilos?"

"Yeah. I think I'm fucked. Look, I ain't one of them fallin'-in-love-ass niggas, but I care about you. A lot. That's why I'm tellin' you this. And I brought you to this studio because you the most perfect woman I ever met. I know you take a lot of pictures on Facebook, but I feel like you need a professional to fully capture yo' perfection. So I want you to take some professional pictures for me. Somethin' I can take wit' me when they lock them doors in my face."

Shanice wrapped her arms around C-Note and cried. "Yes, I'll do it. I'll do anything for you. You the realest nigga I ever met. Damn, I wish we could run away together. I don't want you to go to jail. I need you. I love you."

Hearing those three words left C-Note speechless. He knew she was feeling him, but love was another realm. It made everything more complicated. She had a man. And a baby. And a crazy-ass cousin. They had been stealing time together whenever they could, creeping around for eight months. But the confession had upped the ante. It wasn't about good sex and a good time anymore. It was about love.

"Damn, Shanice. Why you have to say that?"

"Because I want you to know how I feel. I want to be with you. You make me feel how a woman is supposed to feel. Loved. Appreciated. Satisfied. If you leave, I'ma go back to bein' miserable. My time with you is the highlight of my week. Hearin' yo' voice make my day brighter. Seein' yo' face makes me smile. I love you."

"But you got a man. And what about Pop?"

"I don't know, and I don't care. If you want, we can face them both. I just know I want to spend more time with you."

C-Note lay his head against the headrest and closed his eyes. Her words were real. She would face the nigga she built a family with and a stone-cold killer on his behalf. But he knew that would be unfair. He was going to prison, possibly for a long time. Destroying her life and relationships wouldn't be right. Especially if he couldn't be there for her. "I can't let you do that. Not now. I can't let you destroy yo' life while I sit locked up."

"So, what are we going to do? Do you love me?"

When C-Note opened his eyes, Shanice was staring at his face, searching. "I do. For real. And because I love you, I won't let you fuck yo' life up."

"So, again, what are we goin' to do?" she asked.

"I know it's hard, but I think we gotta keep doin' what we been doin' until I put this shit behind me. That's the only way to make sure you'll be okay."

Shanice thought about his words. "You right. I don't want you to be, but damn, you right. I wish you could be wrong or selfish. That's what make you a good nigga. Damn, I wish I woulda met you before I got pregnant by Nitty."

"You wouldn't know pleasure without pain. Winter makes you appreciate summer."

Shanice laughed, wiping the tears from her eyes. "Whatever, street philosopher. You made me mess up my makeup. I hope they got a makeup artist in here."

***

C-Note stared out the picture window of his office overlooking Lux. From the second floor window he could see every square foot of the empty strip club, except the back rooms where the girls groomed, showered, and rested. It was four in the morning, and the club was closed. The only people inside were in his office. Beast Mode, Trench, and Pop Somethin' were sitting around on the couches.

"Permits, licenses, and a couple safety classes. That should cover us so we can all be strapped," Beast Mode said. The name fit the big man perfectly. Six feet tall and 300 pounds. He wasn't muscular, but that didn't make him any less intimidating. At thirty years old, he had jet-black skin, beady eyes, big lips, and hair cut into a Mohawk.

"I got all my paperwork," Trench spoke up. "I'm just waitin' on the green light. My 10-millimeter love takin' chunks outta niggas," he laughed. Trench wasn't as big as Beast Mode, five-foot-ten and 180 pounds, but the bald-headed albino was lethal. Ten years in the military had

A GANGSTER'S CODE

trained him in firearms and battle tactics. He also studied Jujitsu and Kendo, earning black belts. Now at thirty-six years old, he was a pale-skinned killing machine.

"A'ight. I already sent my lawyers to holla at the mayor. We should know somethin' real soon," C-Note said, still looking out the window.

"A'ight. Dolla, dolla bill!" Trench crackled. "We gon' fuck dem country boys up if dey come back in here."

"You got Playa's Club jokes, huh?" C-Note laughed, spinning to face his goons. "Ol' wombat-lookin'-ass nigga."

Beast Mode busted out laughing. "Damn, C-Note! Why you do 'im like that?"

Trench turned on Beast Mode. "I know yo' big ass ain't laughin', over there lookin' like a big-ass mucus ball from the Mucinex commercial."

Everybody in the room laughed, even Pop Somethin'.

"'Bout time you showed yo' human side, Pop. You way too serious, bruh," C-Note said.

"Niggas get killed for playin' too much, but that shit was funny," Pop laughed. "You take care of them books yet? I'm ready to go. I got shit to do."

"Like fuck them fine-ass twins!" Beast Mode said. "Damn, Pop. How you get both of 'em? I seen a lot of crazy shit in these clubs, but I ain't neva seen a nigga fuckin' sisters. What the secret is?"

"Ain't no secret, big homie. I'm just me. Bitches love a real nigga,"

"I'm as real as they come, and I can't even get two bitches to live wit' me, let alone sisters."

"'Cause you ain't me," Pop laughed. "You ready, Note?"

"Yeah, we can ride. I just wanna know if they freaky. Do they fuck each other?"

"Hell yeah!" Beast Mode jumped in.

Pop shook his head. "Nah, not that I know. But I wouldn't tell you niggas if they did."

Beast Mode, Trench, Pop Somethin', and C-Note walked across the deserted parking lot toward their cars. Nobody noticed the dark-colored sedan parked across the street, blending in with its surroundings. As the Lux staff climbed into their cars, four people climbed out of the sedan. Two had assault rifles, one had a shotgun, and the other held two pistols. They took aim at their unsuspecting victims and unleashed hell.

Rat-a-tat-a-tat-a-tat-a-tat!
Boom, boom, boom, boom, boom!
Pop-pop-pop-pop-pop-pop-pop!

When the first shot was fired, Pop Somethin's instincts kicked in. He flinched, ducked, and dove as a bullet hit him in the chest. A burning pain singed his pectoral, but he ignored it, executing a perfect tuck-roll and grabbing both 45s from his shoulder holsters. Before finishing the role, he had already identified the ambushers. Four gunmen stood next to a car about a hundred feet away. All were firing weapons. Pop came out of the roll with both guns blazing, taking aim at his attackers as he sought cover behind his truck.

Beast Mode was the first casualty. The big man's instincts were too slow. A 12-gauge slug hit him in the stomach, making him stumble backward. The second slug hit him in the chest, felling the big fella.

Trench heard the loud pops as hot metal pierced his stomach. Being in Iraq had honed his survival training, so he allowed his body to go with the momentum the bullet

A GANGSTER'S CODE

to his gut had created. He twirled and crouched, pulling the 10 mm as he hit the ground. It only took a split second for him to assess the situation. The machine guns got his attention. Gunfire spattered the ground around him, but he remained calm. He had been trained for war. The 10 mm was his best friend. He took aim at one of the machine gun holders and fired. The ambusher's head snapped back and his body crumpled. The second machine gun shooter got a lock on Trench. The high-powered rifle bullets tore through his body, making him tremble like he was doing the Harlem Shake.

C-Note had just climbed into the Benz when the shooting started. Bullets slammed into the car, shattering windows and sending glass flying. It sounded like they were being ambushed by a small army. The gunfire was loud and rapid. Through the chaos and panic, C-Note managed to pull the Glock from his waist, crawl out of the car, and take cover. He lay on the ground, looking underneath the car to find the shooters. All he could see was their legs. He took aim and fired. Screams filled the night air as two of the ambushers went down. C-Note kept shooting, filling their fallen bodies with hot shit.

Pop Somethin' peeked from behind the Infinity just in time to see C-Note take out two shooters. The last man standing had the shotgun. Pop timed the moment perfectly. When he fired a slug and cocked the pump again, Pop came out from behind the truck squeezing both triggers. The 45 bullets exploded into the man's chest, making him stumble backward, dropping the shotgun as his arms flailed wildly. Bullets laced him from his face to nut sack. Pop looked around, taking in the scene. Bodies covered the ground. He cursed when he seen Beast Mode and Trench.

"Fuck. C-Note, where you at? C-Note?"

"I'm right here," he said, crawling from under the Benz.

"You a'ight, nigga?" Pop asked, rubbing his chest to find the bullet lodged in the Kevlar vest.

"Yeah. I'm good. Is Beast Mode and Trench still alive?"

Pop had a good view of both men. Blood pooled around them and they weren't moving. "Nah, they gone. Let's go look at these niggas' faces."

"You already know who they is. That's ABLE Team."

"I know. I wanna see if Franco or Radar on the ground."

After checking the bodies and not finding the ABLE Team leaders, they went back to their cars.

"You know we gotta go on offense now?" Pop asked.

"What's understood need not be spoken."

"Get the fuck outta here. Find an alibi and lay low. I'ma get at you in a minute.

Chapter 14

Two Days Later

Street hustlers and drug dealers were out in full force, moving up and down the block like worker ants. It was a little past seven at night. Kids ran around playing tag and chasing each other with water guns while old folks sat on their porches block-watching. The sight of the dark-skinned beauty made everybody stop what they were doin' and take a look. The hustlers, kids, and old folks ogled the woman who had mastered the art of seduction.

Queenie strolled down the sidewalk like she was the ghetto version of Tyra Banks. She wore a snug white t-shirt that hugged her breasts and showed her toned arms and slim waist. 'Slay' was printed in big letters across the chest. The tight-fitting, super-flare denim bell-bottoms hugged her hips and thighs, showing her hourglass figure. Her sandals slapped against the pavement as she walked, her long dreads swaying with the switch of her hips.

Two dope boys stepped in her path, cutting her off. "Damn, shawty! Where you goin'? Need some help carryin' all dat ass?" one of them asked. He was tall and light-skinned with a mouth filled with gold teeth. His cornrows looked two weeks old, and his clothes were wrinkled like he slept in them.

Queenie smacked her lips and rolled her eyes. "Boy, please!"

"Don't be like dat, baby," the other one spoke. He was short and chubby. He also paid better attention to his appearance because his clothes were fitted, squeaky clean, and hair cut low with a crisp lining. "What my partna meant to say is 'can we help you find where you goin'?'"

Queenie lost some of her attitude, smiling at hustler number two. "I don't know where I am. I'm from Houston. I just got into a fight with my man and he kicked me out the car. Bitch-ass nigga! I hope he die."

"Damn, baby. What wrong wit' da nigga, lettin' someone as bad as you get away? If you was mine, you'd have yo' own shit. E'rythang foreign," he bragged, pointing to a green Jaguar parked at the curb.

Queenie looked at the car like it was a Bentley. "Ooh, I like that car! Is it yours? What kind is it?"

"That's that new Jag, baby. Seventy thousand dollars cash and dey let me drive right off da lot."

"Is you wit' ABLE Team? I heard them niggas be eatin'. They talkin' 'bout ch'all all the way in H-Town."

The chubby baller poked out his chest, ego forcing his lips to speak without thinking. "Hell yeah! Fuck up a check just to have a good time. Fuck dat bum-ass nigga you came wit'. I'm who you should leave wit'."

Queenie smiled, showing all thirty-two teeth as she did a little bounce. "Hey! That's what I'm talkin' 'bout! My name Baby Girl. Who is you?"

"I'm Fats. Dis my block. I run all dis shit."

"And I'm D.G.," the tall one spoke.

Queenie looked at D.G. like he was getting on her nerves before turning back to Fats. "Since I don't know where I'm at, can you help me? I promise I'ma find a way to pay you back for all the trouble."

"It ain't nothin', baby. What chu need? A ride?"

"Yeah. That would be cool. Can you drop me off at my hotel? I'm at the Best Western."

"I got chu, shawty," he said before turning to D.G. "I'm 'bout to roll with shawty. Hit me if you need me."

"Fo' sho, bruh. See if she got a sista or somethin'."

Queenie ignored D.G.'s comment as she sashayed to the passenger side of the Jaguar. Fats hit the alarm on the keychain, popping the locks as he got in the driver's seat. Amazement showed on Queenie's face as she sat in the luxury car's leather seats. "Dayum! This is nice."

"Hand-sewn seats, baby. Shit, this muthafucka can talk and damn near drive by itself. I'ma cut dis air on so yo' fine ass can cool off. You ain't neva been in nothin' foreign, huh?"

Queenie sighed. "Nah. My man don't got no money. He a bum. Drive a old-ass Fusion. I don't know why I still fuck wit' his bum-ass."

"Listen, shawty. I know we just met, but why don't chu fuck wit' cho boy? I treat chu real good. Me and my niggas fuckin' up Dallas. ABLE Team gon' take over the whole o' Texas. Ride wit' me, baby. Fuck yo' nigga. Look at me."

"Damn, Fats. I like the way you talk to me. It get my pussy wet."

"I got a spot we can chill. Smoke somethin'. Pop a bottle. You down?"

"Hell yeah! Turn up!"

Fats was so focused on bragging and trying to get to know Queenie that he didn't notice the black Charger following him. He drove for ten minutes before parking in front of a blue-and-gray house in a rundown neighborhood. The Charger turned onto the same street a few seconds later, driving ahead and parking on the next block.

"Is this yo' house?" Queenie asked.

"Nah. Some of my action shit, where I fuck off to chill sometimes. I turned the basement into my own li'l spot. It's clean and comfy."

Fats used a key to let them in through the back door. An older, dark-skinned woman appeared at the top of the stairwell. She was rail-thin and had blotchy brown skin and hair nappier than the back of a sheep's ass.

"Damn, Tracy. What, cho ass got super hearin' or somethin'?"

"Hell yeah, nigga. 'Specially when somebody comin' in my house. I was wonderin' when yo' ass was gon' come back through here. Who yo' friend?"

"Dis Baby Girl. I'ma be in the basement. Don't come down here fuckin' wit' us," he said, handing her two bags of dope.

"I got what I wanted. Have fun," Tracy said before disappearing into the house.

Fats led Queenie into a sparsely-furnished basement that was cleaner than expected. Throw rugs of all shapes, sizes, and colors covered the floor. There was a table with a few chairs around it. A small refrigerator was sitting on a shelf in the corner. A couch lined the wall, and there was a bed, as well as a 19" TV on the wall with a video game console and DVD player hooked up to it.

"Is that a waterbed?" Queenie asked.

"Hell yeah. Throwback shit. What chu know 'bout dat?" Fats asked, falling backward on the bed and letting the waves rock his body. Queenie joined him on the bed, giggling as the waves tossed them.

"You want anything to drink? I got some Rosé and Amsterdam in the icebox."

"Yeah. Rosé. You got some strong?"

He tossed her a sack of weed and a wrap as he went to get the drinks.

"You got any movies? Where the porn at?" Queenie asked, rolling the blunt.

"Look in that pile of games."

"Can you do it? I need to call my sister and let her know I'm safe."

"Fo' sho. Do dat. You definitely safe wit' me."

Queenie pulled out her phone and called Princess. "Hey, sis. Yeah, I'm good. I met this nigga, Fats. He fine, and he runnin' up a check. We by his trap house. Finna pop a bottle and smoke some loud."

Fats smiled at the words as he put on the porno.

"Fats, my sister wanna know if she can catch a ride over here and chill wit' us? She at the hotel by herself and bored."

"Yeah, she can come through."

"Here. Talk to her and give her the address."

After talking to Princess, Fats and Queenie lay on the waterbed, smoking, drinking, and watching the porno. When he got touchy-feely, she let him get his feel on, but that was as far as she let him go. Twenty minutes later there was a knock on the back door.

"Tracy, get the do'!" Fats yelled.

Queenie could hear the door open and multiple footsteps on the stairs.

Tracy came into view first. She looked terrified. Fats noticed the look on her face. "Fuck wrong wit' chu?" he asked.

Tracy didn't speak. Behind her was Princess, dressed in a black cat suit, her dreads hanging loose. Excitement shown in Fats' eyes. He was about to comment on them being twins when he noticed Pop Somethin'. The big man wore all black, full beard and dreads hiding most of his face, making him look like the grim reaper. He stood before Fats holding a Sig Sauer 357.

"Awe, c'mon, man! What kinda shit is dis?" Fats whined, the terror setting in.

"I don't got no time for bullshit. Where the fuck is Radar and Franco?" Pop demanded.

"I-I don't got nuthin' to do wit' dem niggas. I just sell a li'l dope," he stammered.

Queenie wore a confused look. "Wait, baby. I thought you was ABLE Team?" she asked, rubbing his belly and grabbing his dick. "It was just hard a couple minutes ago. What happened? I thought ABLE Team was takin' over Texas."

He looked over at Queenie like she was crazy, and then back to Pop Somethin'. "Nah, bruh. I'm not ABLE Team."

Pop reached his arm back and brought the big handgun down across Fats' face. A welt formed on his cheek as blood gushed from the wound. "I'm not gon' ask yo' bitch-ass again! Where the fuck is Franco and Radar?"

"C-mon, bruh! I don't know. I'm a worker."

"What?" Queenie yelled, faking outrage. "I thought you was a baller, baby? I thought you fuck up a check to have a good time? You mean to tell me you just a worker? Ol' lyin'-ass nigga!"

Fats didn't know what to do. He was being taunted by Queenie and attacked by Pop Somethin'.

"Is you ABLE Team?" Pop asked.

"Y-yeah."

"How you get in contact wit' Franco?"

"I call him when I need work."

"Call him. Put it on speaker phone. Tell him you need some work."

Fats visibly trembled as he called Franco.

"Fats! What's good, my nigga?" Franco answered.

"Yo, I need you to ride down on me."

"Damn. Already?"

"Yeah, bruh. The block quackin'."

"Look, I ain't in Dallas right now. I got into some shit and had to move the fam for a li'l while. Niggas plottin' on my head. But I'ma take care of you. Ace and Radar gon' ride down on you. Keep yo' phone on."

After Fats hung up, Pop took the phone and then turned to Princess. "Trial by fire. Let's go."

Princess' body trembled like she was standing in a Midwest winter with no clothes on. She had never fired a gun, let alone shot someone. Pop Somethin' called it a trial by fire. She had to prove her loyalty. This was a test, one she didn't think she would pass. The small six-shot, 32 caliber revolver felt heavy in her hand. She tried to lift her arm, but couldn't.

"I can't do it, Pop," she confessed.

Tracy spoke up. "P-please don't kill me. I won't say nuthin' to nobody."

"C'mon, bruh. I got money. You can have it. The Jag, too. Fuck ABLE Team. I don't like them niggas anyway," Fats pleaded.

Pop ignored both of them, eyeing Princess. "This what we do. No witnesses. The first time is the hardest. Show us you wit' us. Handle yo' business."

"C'mon, Princess," Queenie encouraged. "Don't think about it. Just do it."

Princess' arm shook as she pointed the gun at Tracy. The dope fiend closed her eyes tight and lowered her head, waiting for the boom.

"I can't do it," Princess said, lowering the gun.

Queenie got up from the bed and approached her sister. "Gimme the gun. I'ma show you."

After taking the revolver, Queenie pointed it at Fats' head and squeezed the trigger. *Pop*! Tracy let out a yelp. Princess flinched. Fats' eyes showed surprise as his head snapped back. Blood leaked down his face from a small hole in his forehead as he fell back onto the waterbed.

"See? It's easy," Queenie said, holding the gun out for her sister.

Princess looked to her sister for a sign of fear or remorse. Queenie smiled back at her sister. Killing was easy. At that moment, Princess realized she was wrong about her sister. Not only was Queenie a killer, but she liked it.

When she couldn't stand the joy of killing in her sister's eyes anymore, Princess turned to Fats. The chubby hustler was dead. Blood pooled around his head and his eyes were still open, face flat, devoid of life. The sight made her stomach bubble. She turned to Tracy and seen the dope fiend shaking with fear. She took the gun from Queenie, closing her eyes as she pointed it at the addict's face.

Pop!

The kick from the gun scared Princess and she dropped the gun. When she opened her eyes, the addict was lying on the ground with a hole in her nose, the revolver next to her body. The sight made Princess lose the contents of her stomach.

Pop laughed. "Don't talk about Queenie stomach no more. You the one that can't hang on."

"Fuck you, Pop," Princess managed between heaves. "You muthafuckas crazy."

Chapter 15

Princess lay on the backseat of the Charger, curled in a fetal position. Her eyes were wide open and she was staring at the back of the passenger seat. She kept replaying the scene in her mind. Queenie killed Fats like it was nothing, smiling and playing during and after the murder. She could smell the blood and gunpowder still, see the blood dripping from the dope fiend's face. She had killed someone. Taken a life. Committed a great evil. And now she felt marked.

Queenie poked her head over the passenger seat. "You okay, sis?"

"Hell nah! We just killed two people and burned down they house. Y'all actin' like this shit normal. We done let Pop Somethin' turn us into killas."

"We don't leave no witnesses," Pop cut in, watching Princess in the rearview mirror. "I told you the plan before you got in the car. Now we bound by blood."

"Y'all crazy," Princess whined.

"Don't killin' make you feel powerful? Like a goddess?" Queenie asked.

"Nah. It make me feel like I'm goin' to hell."

"Where all that tough shit at now?" Pop laughed, pulling the car into the gas station. "We killas. Niggas tried to whack me. We gotta bury they ass. That's what we do. This what we in Dallas for. Killin' ain't no different than robbery in the eyes of God. Sin is sin. We can't have you throwin' up every time we body a nigga, so I need you to get it together. I need you to be a souljah. Y'all can talk about it while I go pay for this gas."

When Pop got out of the car, Princess sat up, mugging her sister. "What the fuck you got me in, Queenie? That nigga is crazy as fuck!"

"He not crazy. This what we do."

"What you mean? Listen to how you sound ? Y'all kill people? This not normal."

"Neither is robbing people. I know how it sound. Shit, what's the difference between what we was doin' wit' Pop Squad? Don't act like they wasn't killin' niggas. Ain't no sin bigger than another,."

"But we wasn't part of that shit! The blood wasn't on our hands. We just got the money. Now Pop got us pullin' triggers. That lady didn't do nothin'."

"No witnesses," Queenie said coldly.

Princess cut her eyes at her sister. "You sound like him. What the fuck he do to you? The dick is good, but it ain't that damn good."

"It's not about the dick, Princess. Pop is our nigga. I believe in him and what he stand for. We gotta do what we gotta do to get our goal. In a couple months we gon' be in Jamaica livin' good. Everybody that we kill deserve to die."

"But what about that lady? And what if niggas wit' they kids? Y'all kill babies, too?"

Queenie looked out the window as thoughts of Pop Somethin' smothering Scrap's baby played in her mind. "Collateral damage."

"For real, Queenie? This how you really feel, or is these Pop's words?"

"They mine. Killin' make me feel powerful. Like a god. It get my pussy wet and make me horny. I'm doin' what I wanna do."

Princess stared at her sister like she was seeing her for the first time. "I feel like I don't even know you. I never heard you talk like this. Where is all this coming from?"

"From me. You know for all our life it's been me and you. This is new. I just discovered I can do more. And I want you to be with me. With us."

"I don't like this shit. For real, Queenie. I think we should get away from him. He crazy, and he makin' you crazy."

"And do what? Go back to strippin' and runnin' wit' Pop Squad? I wanna leave the hood and move to Jamaica. What we doin' is temporary. We not gon' kill people forever. This a means to an end. And I'm stayin'."

Princess mugged Queenie. "So you choosin' him over me?"

"C'mon, sis. It's not like that. I love you and want you wit' us. It's gon' get better. I promise, trust me. In a few months we won't have to strip or rob or kill no more. We chasin' a million dollars. That shit gon' change our lives. A mil! Stay wit' us. Please."

The sisters had a stare-down. Princess eventually gave in. "Okay. I can't let you stay wit' this crazy-ass nigga by yo'self."

Pop hopped back in the car and interrupted the sisters' conversation. He spun to face Princess. "So, what's the move? You wit' us?"

Princess rolled her eyes and sucked her teeth. "Yeah, I'm wit' y'all."

"Good. 'Cause I just got a text on Fat's phone. They waitin' on us right now."

***

The sun was setting in the western skyline, giving the horizon an orange hue and purple tint. The colorful sky reflected off the black Yukon Denali that sat idling in a parking space. Radar watched the sun set while using his peripheral vision to keep an eye on their surroundings. The restaurant's parking lot was mostly empty except for a few cars. Paola's was a small Mexican restaurant that didn't have much traffic. It also didn't have any security cameras in the parking lot.

"How can the world be so fucked up, but at the same time give us beautiful shit like sunsets?" Radar asked, exhaling a cloud of weed smoke.

Ace stopped rapping along with Wale and eyed his longtime friend. "What the fuck is you talkin' 'bout, nigga?"

"I'm talkin' 'bout the sunset, nigga. That shit is beautiful."

The setting sun reflected off Ace's platinum teeth as he let his head back to laugh. The six-foot-four, light-skinned goon laughed for a full minute. "What the fuck you just say, nigga? Damn, you say some of the craziest shit, bruh! Who give a fuck about sunsets? How you go from talkin' 'bout poppin' niggas to talkin' 'bout the beauty of a sun? You crazy, bruh."

"I ain't crazy, nigga. This world so fucked up and I try to 'preciate the little things. E'rythang can't be 'bout murderin' and killin'. Niggas gotta have balance. That's the key to life. I know –"

Radar stopped talking when the black Charger pulled into the parking lot. Ace noticed the car at the same time. "You see that, Radar?"

"Yep. Second time they pulled in here," Radar said, pulling the Mac-90 semiautomatic rifle onto his lap.

A GANGSTER'S CODE

The sports sedan pulled alongside the big, black SUV and parked. Princess and Queenie stepped from the car, their reddish-blonde dread locks swaying loosely. Radar eyed the twins, trying to remember why they looked familiar. Ace, on the other hand, had fallen in love.

"Damn! Them hos bad!" he said, tapping on the horn.

The sisters spun toward the truck when they heard the horn. Ace let down his window and waved them over. "Aye! C'mere, shawty. Lemme holla at chu!"

The twins glanced at each other before Princess spoke. "Nah. You get out and come talk to us. Y'all got tinted windows. We don't know what y'all got goin' on in there."

"It's just me and my main man. We waitin' on somebody. C'mere. I don't bite. Unless you want me to."

After one more look, the sisters approached the driver's side of the truck. Queenie nodded. "What up?"

"Yo' thick ass. Why y'all goin' to eat this nasty-ass food? You know they be cookin' dogs an' shit," Ace laughed.

Princess gave an irritated look. "You call us over here to talk shit about our food?"

"Nawl. Chill, shawty. Damn. You know you bad, so you can act up, huh? I ain't neva seen no finer twins in all of Texas. I'm Ace. This my nigga, Radar.".

The sisters blushed at the compliment before Queenie spoke up. "I'm Alexis. This my sister, Mercedes."

"Ooh! I love foreign!" Ace laughed.

The twins laughed with him, but Radar stayed serious, letting the women see he had the gun on his lap. "I seen y'all before. Where I know you from?"

"Aye, chill, nigga! Put that down," Ace said, mugging Radar.

Radar eyed the sisters suspiciously as he slid the chopper under the seat.

"Y'all don't know us," Queenie said. "We from Houston, in town for the weekend."

"That's good. Look, my nigga a li'l high strung, but it's all good. Since y'all only in town for the weekend, take my number and hit me later. I can show y'all the town. ABLE Team own all this shit. I'm the mayor," Ace bragged.

While the light-skinned shooter was still speaking, the back door of the Charger was opening. Ace didn't notice, but Radar did. When he seen Pop's dreads, beard, and muscles, recognition flashed in his mind, and he remembered seeing Queenie with C-Note.

"That's him! That's him!" Radar warned, reaching for the rifle again.

Queenie was ready. Before Radar could get the rifle up, she had pulled the 32 caliber revolver from her purse and pointed it in his face. "Grab it if you want it, nigger."

Radar left the gun on the floor as he stared down the barrel of the little black handgun, but Ace made a move, grabbing Queenie's arm, trying to take the pistol. She began squeezing the trigger, shooting Radar in the leg as he went for the rifle again. Princess ducked. Pop, Somethin' pulled the 357 automatics and started shooting up the truck. Ace let go of Queenie's arm to duck for cover. The female killer seized the opportunity and shot him in the face.

Radar pulled the chopper and started shooting at Queenie. She was able to duck out of the way, so Radar turned his attention to Pop Somethin'. The big man was walking around the truck, filling it with bullets. Radar had a hard time maneuvering the rifle because of the truck seats and the bullet in his thigh, but he kept squeezing the trigger. He managed to spin all the way around, turning his back on the women, and that was his mistake.

A bullet to the back made him fall against the door and drop the rifle. Queenie's face appeared in the driver's window, gun pointed at Radar's face. "I'm tired of tellin' yo' ass to leave that gun alone. Don't touch it no more!"

Radar mugged her, but didn't move.

"Come get him, Pop!" Princess called.

***

"Damn, nigga. You bleedin' all over my fuckin' seats," Pop taunted as he sat next to Radar in the backseat. Queenie watched over the passenger seat. Princess drove.

"Fuck you and yo' seats, nigga!" Radar mugged, barely able to move.

Pop laughed as he reloaded the 357s. "I respect yo' gangsta. Now respect mine and tell me where Franco at."

"Fuck you, nigga! I ain't tellin' you shit. You gon' kill me, or what? This shit hurt."

"Nah, I ain't gon' kill you. Yet. But I'ma make yo' pain worse," Pop said before shooting Radar in the foot.

"Ah! Shit!"

"Tell me what I wanna know, nigga. I know this shit burn. I'ma torture yo' ass 'til you tell me."

"Fuck you, bitch-ass nigga!" Radar yelled, lunging at Pop Somethin'. The movement was slow. Radar was weak from the pain and blood loss, so Pop easily shoved him in the seat and held him down.

"Next one in yo' dick, nigga. Tell me where he at."

Radar hesitated for a moment. He knew a shot to the nuts would hurt like fuck.

And that hesitation was all it took for Pop to squeeze the trigger.

"Ah, shit!" Radar screamed, grabbing his nuts. "Okay! Okay! I'ma tell you where he at. I can't take this shit no more!"

***

"How long we gotta stay here, baby? I wanna go back home. I'm tired of Marcus and his bullshit. And he always lookin' at my ass. That shit creepy."

Franco laughed, slapping and rubbing his wife's ass, "You got a nice ass. Take it as a compliment. All that hard work at the gym is payin' off. Niggas notice."

"But that don't make it okay for yo' brotha to be lookin' at me like that. I wanna go home."

"Chill, baby. Once Radar take care of them niggas, we gon' be outta here. They know where we lay our heads at. I wanna make sure it's safe for us. You know Radar an' 'em don't play. They gon' handle it. We just gotta give it a couple more days."

Michelle sulked as she sat heavily upon the bed. "Y'all shoulda shot his ass while we was in the club. Y'all coulda ended it right there."

"You seen he had security. And cameras and witnesses. The whole team woulda been in jail. We gon' do it the right way. We already lost some good niggas trynna make that last move. They say that big-ass nigga with the beard and dreads is a beast. We gon' find out where all them niggas lay they heads at and bag they ass. These niggas ain't no lames. Shit take a li'l time if you wanna do it right."

"I just wanna go home. Ain't that what you say them niggas for? They supposed to put in work and take the case for you. I want my own bed and bathroom."

The vibrating of his phone took Franco's attention away from his wife. It was a text.

"Who is it?" Michelle asked.

"Radar. He outside. Want me to come out and look at somethin'. He said it's important. I'ma be right back."

Franco walked outside and seen the black Charger with tinted windows parked out front. He walked up and tapped on the passenger window. The window let down slowly. Queenie smiled up at him like she was happy to see him. Franco knew he had seen her before, but he couldn't remember where. When he looked over to the driver's seat and seen the passenger's twin, the hair on the back of his neck stood up. "Where Radar?"

"In the backseat," Queenie said. "Look."

Franco bent down to look in the backseat. What he seen scared the shit out of him and took his breath away. Radar was slumped in the seat, covered in blood. Pop Somethin' sat next to him. He was also covered in blood, dreadlocks and beard hiding most of his face. All Franco could see was his eyes. They were those of a grim reaper. Franco knew he was dead and hadn't even seen a gun yet. Bits of his life flashed in his mind as everything moved in slow motion. Queenie lifted the revolver to his face. He pushed away from the car, attempting to run. Fire sparked from the barrel of the gun, and he could see the bullet fly at his face. His instincts' were no match for the speed of the hot lead. He heard his own scream as the heated metal entered his left eye.

By the time his body hit the ground, he was dead.

J-BLUNT

Chapter 16

The sparkling water ebbed and flowed along the sandy beach, the tide frothy-white like foam atop freshly-tapped beer. Pop Somethin' stood on the shore allowing the waves to flow over his toes. Two weeks had passed since the murder spree when he and his team put down all of their enemies, and now he was standing on a beach in Acapulco, Mexico. Before him, the ocean was vast, and beautiful, and clear blue. There were people all around enjoying the cool water and warm weather, but he didn't notice anyone. In his mind he had been transported back to Jamaica. To Eden. He was a bouncing five-year-old boy again, following in his father's footsteps. He felt the peace, safety, and contentment that came with the innocence of childhood. The smile on his face reflected his inner bliss.

"I never seen you like this. All smiles, too," Princess said, interrupting his thoughts. She stood next to him wearing a pink bathing suit and giant pink sunglasses that covered most of her face, her dreads piled atop her head in a wrap.

"That's 'cause I never felt this close to home."

"Is this what Jamaica's like?"

"Parts of it, yeah. My pops used to take me to this spot called Eden. Bein' here remind me of it. The most beautiful place I ever been. That's where I wanna build the hotel."

The emotion and longing in his voice touched her. "Damn, Pop. You gettin' all sensitive an' shit. Why don't you show this side of you more? You always so serious."

"'Cause niggas will take advantage of you if you show a weakness. Hard shells protect us from the bullshit.

You should feel me more than anybody. I see how you move. You can be cold and calculated when you want to be."

"'Cause I have to be. I had to protect me and Queenie our whole life. It's always been me and her. I had to think for both of us, had to be two steps ahead of these crazy niggas, and three steps ahead of these scheming-ass bitches. Especially in these clubs. Bitches can be worse than niggas."

"Do you still think the worst of me?"

Princess was silent, staring out over the water, watching the people swim. Her eyes landed on Queenie. She was on a surfboard, trying her best to ride the waves. Seeing her sister having fun and being a little girl touched a soft spot inside of Princess. "At first I didn't see what she seen in you. I thought you was a crazy, quick-tempered killa. Which I'm right about, but it's more to you than that. You ambitious wit' dreams and big plans. You real and you smart. And you care about us. We never had nobody like you in our life, so I didn't know how to react when she told me about you or when you asked me to be yo' bitch. But standin' next to you on this beautiful-ass beach, I'm glad I got on the team. I woulda neva did no shit like this if I'da stayed wit' Pop Squad."

"Sometimes we don't know what we missin' 'til we get exposed to it."

Princess smiled. "Preach, baby." They became silent as they watched Queenie splash around in the water. "You know she in love wit' chu, right?"

Pop turned to face Princess. "What about you?"

Princess laughed. "Fuck love. It's about loyalty, right?"

Pop smiled. "Loyalty over everything."

A GANGSTER'S CODE

***

"Is this the life or what, *mi amigos*?" Gonzo smiled, throwing his hands in the air as the wind blew through his clothing. They were on the top deck of his hundred-foot yacht. Pop, C-Note, and a couple bodyguards were lounged around on big-ass couch-like chairs.

"You a boss, Gonzo! A real boss!" C-Note smiled, holding his drink in the air.

"Boss of all bosses!" Pop Somethin' added, holding his drink in the air as well.

"How do you like my homeland? Trump says we're all killers and rapists, no? Then the gringos come to my country to vacation and rape our *señoritas* and our land. Hypocrites! This is the land of the gods! Ancient civilizations. Land of kings!"

The bodyguards clapped and cheered their boss. C-Note and Pop Somethin' egged him on.

"How much it's gon' cost me to get me one of these yachts?" C-Note asked.

"Millions, *mi amigo*. Many millions. Stay with me and one day you and Shooter will have big boats."

"I'm wit' chu to the end!" Pop saluted.

"I wanna see a lab, Gonzo. Show me how y'all make that dope before it get to America. I need to see how to run an operation 'cause I want my own one day. Gimme the game, boss."

Gonzo studied C-Note for a moment. "I normally don't do this, but for you and Shooter, since you save my life, I will show you my farm in Tijuana before we leave. Now, how about we go get some girls from downstairs and swim with the sharks? This is what real men do."

Pop and C-Note looked at him like he was crazy. He noticed their faces.

"What? You no swim with sharks?"

C-Note spoke first. "Hell nah!"

"We black," Pop added. "Niggas don't do that shit. I seen *Jaws*. You know why you don't never see black people in the news gettin' killed by sharks? 'Cause we don't swim wit' no damn sharks."

Gonzo laughed until his stomach was hurting. "You guys have no *cojones*. Wussies. You kill ten people and don't blink, but won't swim in the ocean. I don't understand."

"And you won't. 'Cause we ain't goin'," C-Note said.

"Okay, okay. We just get the women and party. You softies. But before we get too drunk and I forget, Shooter, I need you to take care of somethin' for me in New Orleans. Someone needs to swim wit' the sharks. I can't have it connected to me, which means I can't send my men. Your black skin is an asset."

"Just say when, boss. I got chu."

***

Pop Somethin' stumbled down the hallway toward his room, staggering and bouncing off the walls. He was beyond fucked up, beer, tequila, and cacao in hand, his head spinning and balance thrown off. Partying with the cartel boss was a blast, but stumblin' down the hallway reminded him why he stayed sober.

When he got to his room, sounds from behind the door made him pause. He closed his eyes and shook his head, trying to clear his mind. Then he listened again. Queenie's moans floated up to his ears. Who was she fucking? One of the Mexicans? C-Note? He tried the door, but it was locked.

Queenie's moans stopped after he knocked. "Who is it?" Princess called.

"Me. Open the door."

When the door opened, Pop Somethin' stepped into the room and looked around. Princess stood next to him, naked, her body covered in sweat, breathing heavily, eyes low and red. Queenie was in bed covered in a sheet. She was also sweating and breathing hard. The table next to the bed had a plate on it. It was filled with white powder.

"Who else in here?" Pop asked.

Princess got defensive. "Nobody. Why? What the fuck you talkin' 'bout?"

Pop smiled at Queenie. "Twins wit' a special bond, huh? I guess the time is right, ain't it?"

Queenie threw the sheet aside, exposing her nakedness as she lay back on the bed. "I guess it is. Now you know our secret.

Pop started taking off his clothes. "I ain't trippin'. I just wish y'all woulda told me sooner."

***

The black Toyota C-HR parked in the lot of the law firm. At 6:34 p.m. the door of Hernandez and Jacobs opened and a short Mexican man walked outside. He walked across the lot to a blue BMW. Ten minutes later the driver of the BMW stopped at a Dunkin Doughnuts. Pop Somethin' pulled the C-HR into the lot and watched as the lawyer bought snacks. From the doughnut shop, Pop trailed the defense attorney to the house he shared with his wife and two small children. Hector Martinez was an up-and-comer in the world of law. He was also on Gonzo's shit list. The boss man wanted him dead, so he gave Pop fifty thousand dollars and told him to make it look like a robbery gone wrong. According to the big time dealer, Martinez had purposely lost the trials of some of his workers. He said the lawyer might be working with the feds.

Before Pop made the hit, he wanted to tail the shark for a couple of days to see if he was really working with the feds. The one thing he didn't want to do was be seen or recorded by the feds killing one of their informants. This was day two of the stake out, and so far the Mexican lived a normal life. He went to work, came home, and spent time with his family.

After watching the house for a couple hours, Pop went back to his hotel.

The next morning Pop got up at five a.m. and drove to Hector Martinez's house. As usual, the Mexican left at six and drove to work. At ten, him and a few coworkers took a lunch break, then another break at two. At six he left the firm, heading for home. During the drive, Pop decided tonight would be the night for the kill. After three days of tailing, there was no sign of the feds.

When the BMW pulled into the gas station, Pop drove the C-HR into the parking lot of the super store next door. He tucked the 38 Special in his waist and pulled on the hoody. The plan was to make it look like a car jacking gone wrong. As he walked toward the parking lot, he was happy there weren't many cars or people around.

Hector walked out of the gas station with his face in his phone, oblivious to the danger a few feet away. Pop was reaching for the revolver when a white Camry pulled into the gas station behind Hector's BMW. Pop locked eyes with the Camry's driver. It only took a split second for recognition to set in. He took his hand off the gun as the female climbed from the car. She wore a smile as big as the Saint Louis Arch.

"Crabtree, is that you?" she asked excitedly.

"Nurse Baccara!" Pop grinned, opening his arms for a hug.

Hector looked up from his phone as the sexy Latina hugged the big black man dressed in dark clothes. When he locked eyes with Pop Somethin', he quickly looked away, frightened by the big man's intense stare.

"This is such a small world, Crabtree. What are you doin' in New Orleans?" she asked, stepping back and lookin' him from head to toe.

"The first thing I need you to do is stop calling me my government. It's Pop Somethin'. Pop for short."

She smirked. "I forgot about the infamous Pop Somethin' label. Okay, Pop. How are you. What have you been up to?"

"Trynna stay free. What chu doin' in the N.O.?"

"Oh, just visiting."

Pop waited on her to say more. She didn't. He quickly connected the dots. "You here wit' yo' man, huh?"

She looked surprised. "Yeah. How did you know?"

"Lucky guess. But it don't matter to me if it don't matter to you. I meant everything I said when I used to come see you. This gotta be a sign we was meant to keep each other company, huh?"

She blushed. "I forgot how good you were with your words."

Pop lost his train of though when the lawyer got in the BMW and pulled away. His eyes followed the car. She noticed.

"You okay?"

"Yeah. Uh, I like that car."

She gave him a look that let him know she knew he wan lying. "So, what are you doing here? You still live in Texas, right?"

"Yeah. I'm here on business."

She waited for him to say more. When he didn't, she got the hint. "How long are you in town?"

"Another day. Maybe two. What about you?"

"Hopefully not too much longer. I miss my cat."

Pop laughed. "I forgot you were a cat person. How is Mittens doing?"

The nurse's face lit up. "I can't believe you remembered her name. I'm impressed. She's good."

"I remember everything we talked about. How 'bout we exchange numbers? Do some catching up later on? And who knows, if the situation allows, we might be able to fully act out our moments in those exam rooms."

After exchanging information and a long hug, during which Pop cupped her booty like it was a grocery bag, they parted ways. During the ride back to his hotel, Pop called Shanice to check in on her. She answered the phone sounding down.

"Hey, cousin."

"Why you sound all depressed an' shit?"

She sighed. "Nitty."

Hearing the name made Pop's body temperature rise. "What happened?"

"It don't matter. He gone now."

"Did he put his hands on you?"

"Nah. We just argued."

Pop knew she was lying. "Let's Facetime. I wanna see yo' face."

Shanice got defensive. "Why? I'm good. I told you he didn't hit me."

"Stop playin' wit' me 'fore I come over there."

Shanice didn't respond.

"Shanice!"

"Okay. Okay. Pop, please don't hurt my baby daddy. Don't do my daughter like that."

"What did I tell you? Why the fuck you still lettin' that nigga put his hands on you? I told that nigga I was gon' fuck him up."

She started crying. "Please, cousin. My daughter need her father."

Hearing the emotion in her voice had an effect on Pop Somethin'. He didn't want to add to his cousin's pain. "A'ight."

"A'ight what? Please, Pop. Don't hurt him."

"I ain't gon' touch him. I'm in New Orleans right now, and I couldn't touch him if I wanted to. But you betta quit fuckin' wit' that niggas, 'cause I ain't givin' no more passes."

"I know. It's just complicated. When you love somebody, it makes everything harder."

"Well, you betta un-love his bitch-ass. I'ma check on you when I get back to Texas. If he there, I'm on his ass."

After hanging up the phone, Pop called Queenie.

"Hey, baby. You on yo' way hack home yet?"

"Nah. Not yet. Maybe anotha day or two. I need you and Princess to take care of somethin' for me."

"You know I got you, baby. What you want me to do?"

J-BLUNT

Chapter 17

"I been havin' dreams of killin' a nigga while we fuckin'."

Princess took her eyes off the road and looked over at her twin sister like she was crazy. "Bitch, what the fuck you just say?"

Queenie finished typing the text before setting her phone on the dashboard. "You think I'm crazy, don't you?"

"Who does that? Who has dreams about killin' people they fuckin'? Was it Pop?"

"Nah. They never have faces."

Princess shook her head. "What the fuck Pop do to you? You used to be quiet and naive. Now you just like him."

"Since I been with him, I feel so alive. Like I can be anything and do anything. I never felt like this before."

"That's 'cause yo' ass is in love."

Queenie blushed and rolled her eyes. "Shut up."

"I'm serious. I know you love Pop. He do, too. You know he not gon' be in love wit' you back, right?"

Queenie sighed deeply, staring out the window at the traffic. "I know. And it don't really matter. I mean, it do, but I know Pop. He not wit' that romance and love shit. All he want is loyalty."

"You ever talk to him about love?"

"Not really. It never really came up."

"It might not be a bad conversation to have when he get back in town. Is this the house right here?"

Queenie looked up at the red and blue house. "Yeah. That's his truck right there. Park a couple houses away."

"So, what we gon' do? Walk up to the house and call him outside and say let's talk?"

"Nope. He should be out any second. That was him I was just textin'."

"How you get his number?"

"I made a fake Instagram and Facebook right after I talked to Po. This nigga liked all my pictures. Look." Queenie showed Princess her phone. The pictures made her eyes pop.

"Girl, you don't look nothin' like Skittlez. Why you doin' our girl like that?"

"Short notice. You got a better plan?"

"No. But look, there he go. Damn, he big! You sure about this?"

Queenie pulled the 357 from the glove compartment and smiled. "I neva met a nigga that was bulletproof."

When the blue Suburban pulled away from the curb, Princess trailed him in the rented Buick Lacrosse. They stopped in a Walmart parking lot a couple minutes later. Queenie's phone buzzed. It was a text.

"He ready for me. Wish me luck."

Princess looked worried. "You sure you don't want me to come wit' chu? That nigga big and look crazy."

Queenie stuffed the revolver into her Prada clutch as she climbed from the car. "Chill, sis. I got this."

Queenie left the rented Buick dressed in a tight-fitting black t-shirt, a black mini-skirt, and heels. She powerwalked toward the Suburban, stopping at the passenger door and knocking on the window.

When the driver seen her, a million questions showed on his face as he lowered the window. "What up?"

Queenie smiled up at him like he won a prize on a game show. "Hey, Nitty. It's nice to meet you in person."

He frowned. "I know you?"

"Not really, but I'm hopin' we can change that. I'm Star."

Surprise and mistrust showed on his face. "Why you send me a picture of somebody else?"

"I got my reason. Can I get in so we can talk about it?"

Nitty eyed her for a few seconds before nodding. "Yeah. Help me understand why someone as bad as you out here catfishin' niggas."

Queenie could feel Nitty's eyes all over her body as she climbed in the truck. He skirt rose high on her tattooed thighs as she sat in the passenger seat. Nitty watched her struggle to pull it back down over her thickness. "It wasn't like that. I created Star to get Bitcoin money from those internet tricks. I ran up a check doin' that shit. Then, when I seen you in my DM, I remembered you. You still don't know who I am?"

He studied her face, then let his eyes roam across her body again. "You look familiar, but I don't know why."

"I used to fuck wit' Pop Somethin'."

Nitty's face twisted into a mean mug. "I remember you now. You was in my house when that nigga sucka-punched me. Where that ho-nigga at? I'ma fuck his bitch-ass up!"

"I don't know where that nigga at. Fuck him. I don't fuck wit' that nigga no more. I wish you woulda whooped his ass."

"When I catch 'im, I'ma blaze 'im. That's my word!"

"Good. He got that comin'. But fuck him. Like I was sayin', when you DMed me, I remembered you and I thought you was sexy as fuck. I didn't wanna blow up my hustle, so I had to lie a li'l bit. I wasn't trynna set you up or nothin'. I just didn't wanna fuck up my hustle."

Nitty smiled, satisfied with the explanation. "So, them niggas online be cashin' you out, huh?"

"You'd be surprised what a nigga do for a pussy picture," she laughed.

Nitty looked over her body lustfully, his eyes resting on her thighs. "Fuck a picture. I need the real thang."

Queenie gave him a sexy stare. "That could be arranged."

Nitty smiled. "On what?"

"I don't believe in promises. I believe in blue cheese."

"A dollar, huh? Okay. I'ma play. Where we goin'?"

Queenie looked toward the backseat. "How long you wanna play? Yo' backseat look big enough to go a couple rounds in."

"Lemme find somewhere to park."

While Nitty drove, Queenie freed his dick from his pants and gave him head. A few minutes later he pulled the suburban into an alley. He was so concerned with busting a nut that he didn't notice the Buick pull into the alley behind him.

Queenie pushed him onto the backseat and pulled a rubber from her purse. After strapping him up, she climbed on top and rode fast and hard. Thoughts of sex and murder had Queenie lost in sexual bliss. Nitty moaned beneath her, palming her ass and enjoying the ride. His eyes were closed and he was so caught up in the sex that he didn't notice Queenie pull the pistol from her purse.

She waited until her orgasm was close. She watched Nitty's face as she rode him. His fuck faces were beyond ugly, like a Saint Bernard mixed with a gorilla.

When she put the pistol to his head and cocked the hammer, his eyes shot open. Fear and confusion shown in them.

Queenie pulled the trigger and came at the same time. Blood spattered across her face as she cried out in ecstasy. The orgasm racked through her body, lasting a full minute, coming in waves. She was delirious with pleasure as she sat on the dead man's lap. She had never felt so good or came so hard. Fucking and killing was the ultimate high.

She stared into his death mask while she caught her breath. His eyes were still open. And blank.

"I'm a goddess," she mumbled before climbing out of the SUV.

***

Pop grunted in frustration, slapping his hand against the C-HR's steering wheel. He had been in New Orleans for seven days, and the way things were looking, he might be stuck there for another day. Hector's BMW sat in the driveway of his house. It hadn't moved in four days since the Mexican left with his family in an Uber for the airport. Pop had checked the house every day to see if the family had returned. Four days in a row he drove away disappointed.

The only good thing that had come from his trip was it gave him an alibi. Shanice called him right after Nitty died, cursing him out. Pop swore he was still out of town. He hadn't heard from his cousin since, but he planned to check up on her as soon as he got back to Texas.

As he drove away from Hector's house, Pop thought about his bitches. Queenie was a beast, a homicidal maniac who got turned on by murder. She was the Yin to his Yang. He didn't' believe in soul mates, but if he did, Queenie was his.

And then there was Princess, his wild card. A headstrong, bad bitch with an unbreakable will. A woman who could separate business from pleasure, sex from emotions, and love from loyalty. She was the flip side of his coin. Together the twins possessed everything he'd ever wanted in a woman. The added bonus being the sisters were also lovers. Somewhere deep inside he knew the incestuous sisters were fucked up in the head, but that didn't bother him enough to stop them from being his bitches.

Vibrating on his lap caused him to abandon thoughts of his ride-or-dies. When he picked up the phone, 'Nurse' was showing on the screen. "What up, Ms. Baccara?" he smiled.

"How come you can call me by my last name, but I can't call you by yours?"

"Because you a professional woman. I use it as a sign of respect. Plus, that shit sound sexy as fuck."

She laughed. "Whatever. But just so you know, my name is Joslyn."

"Nah, that don't turn me on like Ms. Baccara do. I got you in my phone as 'nurse.' That's how I wanna keep it."

"Whatever floats your boat. So, what are you up to?"

"Shit. Been wonderin' when you was gon' call. What you up to?"

"Nothing. Sick and tired of New Orleans. Ready to leave. Tired of this *punta* that calls himself my man."

"I know just the thing to take yo' mind off yo' problems."

"I'm open to suggestions. What you got in mind?"

"Me."

A GANGSTER'S CODE

"C'mon, Pop. Stop playing."

"I ain't playin'. I wanna see you. I dreamed about you the night we met at the gas station. We fucked in the exam room. Since the *punta* is pissin' you off, why don't you come to my hotel room and let me take yo' mind off all yo' problems. I'm good at easin' people's minds."

She was quiet for a few seconds. "You know, hearing you talk like this is making me so horny. I might have to take you up on your offer."

"Might?" Pop questioned. "What the fuck are you waitin' for?"

***

When Pop opened the hotel door, Ms. Baccara stood in the hallway dressed in a pair of tight-fitting pink nurse scrubs. The Columbian beauty wore light make-up, her full lips glossy and wet with red lipstick, her hair piled atop her head in a bun. She walked into the room looking like a mix between Eva Mendez and J-Lo.

Pop grabbed her around the waist and pulled her into his arms. "Girl, getcho fine ass in here!"

They kissed and stripped their way to the bed. By the time they fell atop the covers, they were naked. Pop attacked her body like a hungry animal, manhandling her as they rolled across the bed. The nurse moaned in delight, loving his aggressive nature. Pop wasted no time getting in her guts. Her pussy was tight and wet, and the noises she made had Pop in the zone.

She moaned and clawed his back, loving the deep strokes, wanting more and more. When Pop busted his nut, in the back of his mind he wondered how he would convince Queenie and Princess to make room in their bed for the nurse.

***

On his twelfth day in Louisiana, Pop finally got the moment he had been waiting for. Hector had come back home. Pop trailed the blue BMW to Dunkin Doughnuts. When the Mexican went inside, Pop got in position. Hector walked out of the doughnut shop sipping coffee, holding a bag of sweets. When he made it to his car, he sat the bag of goodies on the roof to dig into his pocket for the keys. Pop timed his approach perfectly. When the lawyer looked up, Pop was only a few feet away, the big revolver pointed at his face. All Hector could do was flinch. At that moment he remembered Pop Somethin' from the gas station. Seeing the fear excited the killer, making him smile.

The lawyer opened his mouth to scream and ended up with a 38 slug in his throat. Two more shots to the face ended his life. He didn't even feel Pop Somethin' take the belongings from his pockets.

Chapter 18

"I feel bad for sayin' this, but maybe God did us a favor. You a good woman, and you been through so much bullshit wit' this nigga. Them church people sing that song about holding they place and letting God fight they battles. They say God work in mysterious ways."

Shanice was sitting on the couch wrapped in C-Note's arms, her head against his chest and sipping a glass of apple juice. They were at her house. Since Nitty died, he slept over twice. His presence comforted her. She wore only a t-shirt. All he had on was boxers.

"It's just hard knowing my daughter won't ever see her father again. I know people die all the time, but you never really know how short life is until you lose someone close to you. Even though Nitty wasn't shit, I still didn't want him to die."

C-Note didn't have anything good to say about Nitty, so he kept quiet.

Shanice spun to face him. "And you know what's crazy? When the detectives told me he was dead, I couldn't stop the tears from falling. I was hurting real bad. And while the hurt was settling in my heart, I felt a sense of relief, too. Like a burden had been lifted from my shoulders. I understand what you meant about God working in mysterious ways, but am I wrong for feeling like this? Like I'm free?"

"Nah, baby. You human. You been abused and taken advantage of, and now yo' abuser is dead. I think you s'posed to feel how you feel. I think it's normal, especially considerin' how that nigga died."

"At first I thought Pop did it. The night before Nitty died, I told Pop he hit me. Soon as I could talk again, I called Pop and cussed his ass out and told him I hated him. Then, a couple days later, they tell me a woman killed him and he died while cheating on me. I felt stupid for doin' my cousin like that. Pop never lied to me my whole life. I shoulda trusted him and believed him when he said he didn't do it."

"Yeah, that nigga don't like to play around. I think I only seen the nigga laugh a handful of times. You should call him. He love yo' ass like you his sister. Yo' words prolly cut him deep."

"I know. I'm kinda scared to call him. And embarrassed."

"Call him. Pop a good nigga."

"I will. But forget about my problems. What's up with your case? Did your lawyers say anything?"

"Yeah. State Attorney offered a deal, but it's bullshit."

A glimmer of hope shown in Shanice's eyes. "What kinda deal?"

"Shit, I can prolly walk, scot-free."

Her face lit up like a Christmas tree. "Oh my God! That is good. Why are you just now telling me this? Why haven't you taken the deal?"

C-Note looked out the window. "It ain't that easy, baby. They want me to snitch."

Shanice's eyes lost some of their light. "Oh," she mumbled. Silence filled the living room until she broke it. "I know you don't want to be looked at as a snitch, but it will keep you out of jail. I mean –"

C-Note chuckled. "That's easy for you to say 'cause you ain't in the game. It's rules to this shit. Snitchin' can get me killed."

"What if we relocate? Move to New York or California? Somewhere away from Texas."

"I'm fuckin' wit' a cartel boss. You can't outrun them. Or Pop. That nigga believe in the rules to the game as much as I do. He would prolly kill me if I snitch."

"But I love you, C-Note. You the best thing that ever happened to me. I need you. Now that Nitty is dead, we can be together. Like you said, God did us this favor. We should take advantage of it."

"C'mon, Shanice. I just told you it ain't that easy."

"Do you love me? Love is an action where you make sacrifices for people you love. I would rather be on the run with you for the rest of my life than be apart from you for ten or twenty years. Please, C-Note. Think about us."

C-Note shook his head, unable to speak. He loved Shanice, but snitching on Gonzo was out of the question.

Shanice read his body language. C-Note was sticking to his guns. She lowered her head and began playing with her glass of juice. Then she mumbled, "I'm pregnant."

Her words took a couple seconds to register in his mind. "What chu just say?"

Shanice kept her head down. "I missed my period. I'm pregnant."

C-Note's eyes grew wide and his throat got dry. "Baby, you can't be playin' about no shit like this. I know you love me, but don't do this."

Shanice sat her drink on the table and got up from the couch. She went to her room and came back holding two pregnancy tests in her hand. C-Note looked at the tests. Blue plus signs showed on each one.

"Is it mine?"

"I don't know. I'm not sure when it happened. I was still fucking Nitty, too."

"Fuck. I thought you was on birth control."

"I am. I took the shot. It's supposed to last five years, but nothing is one hundred percent."

"Fuck," C-Note cursed and became silent.

Shanice started crying. "I-I-I'm sorry. I didn't mean to make you mad. That's why I didn't want to tell you."

Seeing her cry touched a soft spot inside C-Note. He got up from the couch and wrapped her in his arms. "It's a'ight, baby. I gotchu. We good."

"No, it's not," she cried. "You still mad."

"I'm not mad. This was just unexpected. Shit, I wasn't ready for this."

"Neither was I, but now I'm pregnant and I already got a daughter without a father. Are you gon' leave me, too?"

Her words entered his ears, traveled through his brain, down to his heart, and exploded in his chest. She was pregnant. The baby might be his. They were in love. She needed him. He didn't want to watch his possible seed grow up through pictures and visits.

The tears rolled down his face, mixing with hers. "I'm not gon' leave you, baby. I gotchu."

C-Note's words were instantly comforting. When she looked up and seen his tears, her heart melted. That single act made her love him that much more.

Her lips found his. This kiss was different than any kiss they had ever shared. It was emotional, like their souls were being joined. When C-Note sat on the couch, Shanice took off her shirt and climbed on top. She wasn't wearing any panties. When his dick came through the hole in his boxers, it slipped right into her pussy. The lovebirds kissed and moaned as they made soul-joining love.

A loud crash at the front door made them both freeze up. What they seen took all of the air out of the room and made C-Note's dick go limp.

***

"Fuck this nigga doin' over here?" Pop Somethin' wondered aloud as he parked his brand new, maroon Maserati behind the black Benz truck. It didn't take long for him to answer his own question.

There was a snake in the grass. An un-crossable line had been crossed. He had been betrayed.

The mean mug spread across his face, and the anger warmed his body as he climbed from the luxury sports car. The one thing he didn't play about was family. Seeing C-Note's truck parked out front of Shanice's house made his blood boil. In Pop's mind, C-Note was taking advantage of a situation. His cousin was hurting and needed comforting. C-Note probably used her pain to get his pleasure. His little homie had broken an unwritten and unspoken rule: don't fuck with yo' nigga's family unless you get permission. Period. All rule breakers must pay.

When he walked up on the porch, movement in the window caught his eye. It was Shanice. He could see she wasn't wearing a shirt as her breasts bounced wildly as she rode C-Note on the couch. The faces she made showed a mix of pleasure and pain. For a moment Pop was caught up in the show. Shanice was beautiful. Pop knew she was special the first time he laid eyes on her, back when they were children. She was precious. Regal. A queen. God hadn't created a man good enough to be with her. Actually seeing her fuck C-Note sent a new level of anger coursing through his body, along with something else. Jealousy.

Before he realized what was happening, he pulled the Glock 29 from his waist and kicked open the front door. The sight of Pop Somethin' with a gun made the lovers freeze in terror. In the blink of an eye the big man struck. He pushed Shanice onto the couch. In the same moment he dropped the gun and picked up C-Note, throwing him across the room like a rag doll. The small man flew across the living room and crashed into the wall. Before he could move a muscle, Pop Somethin' was standing over him, dropping heavy lefts arid rights. The blows rained down on C-Note's face and head, knocking him in and out of consciousness.

"*Paul, stop!*" Shanice screamed.

Shanice's scream cut through the living room, the pain and desperation in her voice cutting through Pop's rage and bringing Pop back to reality. C-Note lay on the ground, not moving. His eyes were closed, face rapidly swelling. Seeing the damage calmed Pop a little.

He spun toward Shanice. She held Pop's gun in her hand, pointing it at his chest. The little calm he felt vanished. "You gon' pull a muthafuckin' gun on me for this bitch-ass nigga?"

"Please, stop," Shanice cried. "Leave him alone."

"So, you gon' shoot me? Do it! Shoot me!" Pop screamed, walking toward Shanice.

She hung her head, dropping the gun to put on her t-shirt when she realized she was still naked. Pop snatched the gun up from the floor and put it on his waist.

"This what y'all do? Sneak around? What I tell you 'bout fuckin' wit' these street niggas? You ain't learned yo' lesson from Nitty? These niggas ain't shit. The don't love you. It's all about a nut."

"Not C-Note. He different."

"How? Cause he ain't put his hands on you yet? This nigga finna go to jail. Why you fuckin' wit' a nigga that's finna leave you? You settin' yo'self up to get hurt."

"I don't care about none of that. I love him, and he loves me. That's all that matters."

Confusion showed on Pop's face. "You just buried the nigga you spent five years wit', and now you already in love? Stop playin'." Then realization set in. "Wait. This ain't the first time y'all fucked, huh? How long this been goin' on?"

"Since he got out," she mumbled.

Pop ran a hand across his face in frustration. He told C-Note to check up on his cousin, not fuck her. A line had been crossed. Rules broken. And C-Note hadn't paid enough yet. He spun around to attack the helpless man again when Shanice's words stopped him.

"I'm pregnant."

Pop stopped in his tracks, her words grabbing him. He cut his eyes at her and smirked. "You muthafuckas trippin'."

"I'm a grown woman, Pop. I can make my own decisions. I don't need you watching over me and tellin' me what I can and can't do wit' my body. I want to be with him. We're in love. We want to be a family."

Pop stood there, Shanice's words playing in his mind as he looked back and forth from his cousin to C-Note's unconscious form lying on the floor. He was unsure of what to do. Shanice loved and wanted to be with C-Note. The only way to keep them apart was to kill C-Note. Shanice would probably hate him for that. He was already guilty of killing someone she loved and bringing her pain, and he didn't want to hurt her again. As much as he hated C-Note's deceitfulness, his love for Shanice trumped the ill will. He didn't like what they were doing, nor did he respect it, but he had to accept it. They were grown. Shanice was pregnant. Her baby needed a father. It would be unfair for both her children to be fatherless.

Instead of acting on his anger and stomping a hole in C-Note's ass, he walked toward the door. "Tell that nigga to call me when he wake up."

Chapter 19

One week later

"Look like you been in a fight."

C-Note mugged the older, brown-skinned man that sat across from him. Detective Lawson was a twenty-year vet of the police force. The bald head and thick mustache made him look like a Steve Harvey impersonator. The aggressive stare-down spoke of the hostility between them. The last time he got questioned, he told Lawson the same thing. Now that he had been dragged down to the police station for a third time, he was fed up. His mean mug told of how tired he was of being harassed and questioned, and the look on the detective's face told how tired he was of being lied to.

"Stop playin', man. Fuck you want?" C-Note spat.

"I wanna know what kinda shit you was in that got six bodies piled up outside yo' club? No witnesses. No video. Nothin'. And by the look of yo' face, whoever came to yo' club lookin' for you back then must've recently found you," he laughed.

Multiple bruises covered the young hustler's face. His left eye had a darkened and purple bruise under it, and a bump on the left side of his head was still visible. "I told you that didn't have nothin' to do wit' me. Lux close at three. I was at home wit' my sister and nephews."

"You already told me that. So, what happened to yo' face?"

"I got in a fight."

"Did, you win?"

C-Note shifted uncomfortably. "Yeah."

Lawson burst out laughing "What the other nigga look like? Yo' scrawny ass ain't walkin' away lookin' like that and expectin' me to believe you won."

The hostile look was back in C-Note's eyes. "If that's all the questions you got, then I gotta go. I got a business to run."

"What the feds offer?"

C-Note stood and took a step toward the door. The detective got up and stood in his way. "You in ova ya head, boy! Federal agents. Kilos. Murder. You know you ain't built for what them feds got for ya. Work wit' me. Tell me somethin'. I'll get you a good deal."

"Stop harassin' me, man. I already called my lawyer."

"I know who he is. I met him the last time you was in here. All he doin' is takin' yo' money. Once them feds get their hands on you, they already got you. The only one that can help you is me. Talk to me, son."

Another staring contest took place. It was interrupted by a knock on the door. When it opened, a white officer stuck his head in the room. "His mouthpiece is' here. We gotta cut him loose."

***

Meek Mill's *Holy Ghost* flowed through the expensive speakers of the Benz truck as C-Note stared out at the road, lost in thought. He was in a jam. Feds on one side, Dallas Police on the other. Baby momma in front, her cousin in back. Every time something good happened, something bad followed. That was his life, and it seemed like the more money he got, the more problems came with it. A constant roller coaster ride, and now the ride appeared to be over. Bet big, lose big. C-Note was tired of losing. He needed a win.

The phone vibrating on his lap pushed thoughts of a crashed and burned-out roller coaster from his mind. When he seen the name on the screen, his mind flashed back to a week ago, the day Pop kicked in the door and caught him and Shanice fucking. He didn't remember any of the attack, just woke up with his head in Shanice's lap, his entire body hurting. He waited three days to call Pop. After a long talk, they agreed to let bygones be bygones. C-Note accepted the ass-whooping and Pop accepted him fucking with Shanice.

"What up, bruh?"

"Where you been at, nigga? I been trynna get at you all day," Pop said excitedly.

"Lawson got at me earlier. Tried to put pressure on me. My lawyer got me out that shit. He filing a lawsuit on them for harassin' me. What up wit' chu?"

"The streets is talkin'. Queenie heard some shit. It's serious. We need to holla face-to-face."

"Say no more. I'm on my way."

***

When C-Note pulled to a stop in fron' of Pop's house, the big man climbed in the SUV wearing a serious look. "Gonzo got knocked."

C-Note looked blown away. His eyes popped and jaw dropped. "You bullshittin', bruh. Tell me this some bullshit."

"Nah. This shit might be real. I tried to call him, but his phone off. This shit might be true. Queenie got word from Skittlez. Overheard some niggas last night at some club on the otha side."

C-Note lay his head against the headrest and closed his eyes. An unspeakable emotion was etched across his face. Ups and downs. A constant roller coaster. "Nah, bruh. C'mon, man. This bad luck shit is fuckin' me up. If it ain't one thing, it's anotha."

"I know, my nigga. I feel the same way. We had it good. A plug in Mexico. The plug of all plugs. I hope it ain't true. Gonzo was my nigga."

C-Note opened his eyes and exhaled deeply. "A'ight, I gotta get up wit' Lucci. I was on my way to Lux. What you on?"

"Shit, I'm wit' chu. In case Gonzo hit one of us up, we need to stay together."

The men got lost in thought as C-Note whipped the Benz through traffic. "So, what the next move is?" Pop asked. "If Gonzo really gone, then what? Every move you made on the grind got my pockets right, so I'ma fuck wit' chu. You a real hustla. You know how to make somethin' outta nothin'."

"I don't know, Pop. I don't even wanna think about that shit. I'm still stuck on Gonzo gettin' knocked."

"You thinkin' 'bout callin' it quits? Even though I don't like it, you and cuz about to have a baby. I ain't sorry I whooped yo' ass, but I got love for you, nigga. You already in a fucked up spot. Trynna get greedy might get you in a tighter jam. You got a business and a nice stash. Sometimes you gotta fold yo' hand. Leave wit' somethin' instead of nothin'."

"You know Lawson fag-ass had jokes about my eye," C-Note laughed. "I know I crossed a line, my nigga. I shoulda been real enough to tell you 'bout me and cuz on day one. I know what type of nigga you is. I did this to myself."

"Yeah," Pop agreed, "but we good, my nigga. I fuck wit chu the long way. Now, tell me what you know about investin' money."

"Not much. Gotta talk to Shanice. She s'posed to be lookin' into some accounts for me. She want me to quit trappin'. I'm sittin' on half a ticket. She want me to go legit and set up a future for the kids."

Pop smiled. "Li'l cuz a winner, isn't she?"

C-Note gave Pop a look that told his true feelings. Shanice was more than a winner, more than a dime. She was one in a million, his way out of the streets. Fine and smart. A good woman who waited her whole life for a good nigga.

He was about to brag to Pop about Shanice when something caught the corner of his eye. His foot reacted. The Benz truck jerked, tires skidding as the brakes locked up. Pop Somethin' braced himself for impact. He had seen the Dodge Ram pickup truck at the last moment. The collision couldn't be avoided.

The pickup rammed the Benz, sending both vehicles in a spin-out. As soon as the Ram spun to a stop across the street, the shooting began. Two gunmen hopped out of the truck with M-16s. They sprayed C-Note's truck with bullets, trying to kill the occupants.

A novice to the streets would've died from the high-powered rifle bullets that tore through the Benz's frame, but not Pop Somethin'. His instincts had been honed like that of a soldier on the battlefield. Right before the truck smashed into the Benz, he braced himself. By the time the Benz stopped spinning, his 44-caliber Desert Eagles were out of his shoulder holsters and in his fists. The enemy had choppers, and he had chopper stoppers. Thirteen bullets in each gun was enough to take on anybody. He also had something else that his enemies didn't: the protection of the Benz truck's frame.

When he started firing the hand cannons, loud and powerful booms made his attackers pause, and that was their mistake. In the split second it took them to duck and flinch, Pop got the advantage. He spotted his enemies taking cover. One of them didn't duck low enough. A high-powered 44 bullet hit him in the chest, another in the neck. The last one took a chunk out of his face. He dropped to the ground, his last breath already breathed. The final enemy had the heart of a lion. He' was on a mission and would see it through or die trying. When the 44 slug slammed into his head, he didn't even feel it.

"C-Note! Get up! Let's go," Pop yelled.

Blood leaked from C-Note's nose as he tried to shake the stars from his head. The airbag had burst in his face, dazing him a little. When he came to his senses, Pop Somethin' was dragging him across the passenger seat and out of the truck. "I'm good," he called trying to stop Pop Somethin' from dragging him.

When he seen C-Note was fully conscious, Pop let him go and ran toward a green Jeep that was stopped at a stop sign. C-Note watched the goon bring Grand Theft Auto to life. He snatched open the Jeep door and ripped the woman from the driver's seat like she only weighed ten pounds. C-Note barely had time to close the door before Pop smashed the gas.

"Them niggas was Mexican!" Pop screamed, wiping blood from his face. He had a cut on his jaw where his head went t rough the passenger window.

"I didn't' see 'em. I don't know."

A GANGSTER'S CODE

"I'm not askin' you, nigga. I'm tellin' you. They was Mexican," Pop repeated as he whipped the Jeep through traffic at a high speed.

C-Note looked puzzled. "I didn't see 'em. You sure they was Mexicans?" We don't got no beef wit' them niggas.

Pop glanced over at C-Note, a sure look on his bearded face. "They was Mexican. I been around enough of them niggas in the joint to know one when I see one. Don't tell me you busted Gonzo head. I know you didn't do no bitch-ass shit like that?"

A mix of emotions passed over C-Note's face. Fear. Shock. Anger. "Why you comin' at me like that, bruh? I'm a man. I stand on my own two feet. Don't put that fuck-nigga jacket on me, man. I'm a gangsta. I get down for mine. You know that."

Pop stared at C-Note like he was trying to see through to his soul. "Tell me the truth, nigga. I don't tolerate niggas that snitch. Put it on everything you love that you didn't bust a move on Gonzo."

Tears the size of raindrops welled up in C-Note's eyes. "On everything I love, I didn't tell on Gonzo. I'm takin' my weight, bruh."

Pop turned his attention back to the road. "We gotta get the fuck off these streets. That shit back there got you hotter. I know them people gon' trace that truck back to you. It might be time for you to take yo' money and run, li'l bruh. We burnt up Dallas. Too much bullshit comin' yo' way. Only a matter of time 'fore it get to me."

"Fuck Texas," C-Note agreed. "This shit too much. Go to the playa pad so we can lay low and think of our next move. We gotta get the fuck outta here as soon as possible.

***

"What you think goin' on? Do you believe Pop?" Queenie asked as she and her sister walked up on the porch of their house.

"I don't know. That shit ain't addin' up. When we got ABLE Team out the way, everything was' s'posed to die down. It ain't no coincidence that somebody came at Pop and C-Note. Not after you heard that shit about Gonzo. That nigga opened his mouth. He in love wit' Shanice and trynna save his ass. I'ma tell Pop what I think as soon as we get our shit out this house and get back to him."

The sisters grew quiet as Queenie unlocked the door. Princess looked around outside as they walked in, keeping her eyes open for anything that looked out of the norm. After the sisters made it safely in the house, Queenie locked the door behind them. "I just didn't think it would be over in Dallas. Not this fast. We only been here a couple months, and the money so good. Damn, we was gettin it."

"I know," Princess agreed, "but Pop is a good nigga. The best thing you ever did was ride off wit' his crazy ass. The three of us make a badass team. We can go anywhere and make it happen. We just gotta convince Pop that his boy is a rat so he can terminate his ass. C-Note is a sinkin' ship, and we can't let our nigga go down wit' him."

"Hell yeah. Go grab the guns and money from downstairs. I'ma go to the room and put us some suitcases together."

Queenie went to their bedroom and grabbed three suitcases and threw them open on the bed. She packed one for her, Princess, and Pop Somethin'. Since they didn't have a planned destination and would probably be living out of hotels, she knew she couldn't pack much. The thought of leaving behind thousands of dollars' worth of clothes, appliances, and electronics saddened her. This was the first house she ever felt at home in, and now they had to leave.

Fifteen minutes later she had packed her and Princess' suitcases and was working on Pop's. A loud crash from somewhere in the house scared her. She stopped packing and grabbed the 380 Smith and Wesson from her purse.

"Princess, you good?" Queenie called, walking slowly down the hallway toward the living room. Nobody answered, but she could hear more than one set of footsteps in the house. Queenie stopped in the middle of the hallway and pointed her gun toward the sound of footsteps. A split second later two people dressed in black rounded the corner carrying automatic weapons. The 380 sparked as Queenie emptied the clip. Bodies crumpled to the floor, their consciousness turned off like a light switch.

Queenie was so caught up in the sight and smell of death that she wasn't ready for what came next. Another figure dressed in black jumped out, firing a machine gun. The murderess reacted fast, diving into the bedroom as bullets tore into the wall where she had been standing. After a scramble, she ran to the closet and hid under a pile of clothes.

The floor creaked as someone crept into the room. Whispering Let her know more than one person was looking for her. She was certain they would find and kill her. She wasn't scared of death, but she didn't want to die. She was too young, only twenty years old. She wanted to spend more time with Pop and her sister. She wanted to see Jamaica, experience life.

When the closet door opened, she knew all of her wants and desires would die with her.

Pop-pop-pop-pop-pop-pop-pop-pop-pop-pop-pop-pop!

"Ah!" Queenie screamed as rapid gunfire exploded.

"Queenie! Queenie, where you at?" Princess whispered.

The pile of clothes moved and Queenie came out with wide eyes. Two bodies lay on the floor with blood pooling around them. Princess stood a few feet away holding an M-16, her eyes wide with fear and concern. "You good?"

"Yeah. Damn, bitch. I thought I was dead. You came through."

"I told you I got you, sis. I ain't finna let nothin' happen to you. Now getcho ass up. We gotta get the fuck outta here."

The sisters moved quickly through the house, Princess leading the way with the M-16. Queenie followed, struggling to carry the three suitcases. They were heading for the back door. The money and guns were in duffel bags waiting by the back stairwell.

They had just stepped into the kitchen when the back door came crashing in. Princess jumped into action, spraying the doorway with bullets. The person dressed in black that tried to run in the house was gunned down in a hail of bullets. Since the guns and money bag was near the dead body, the sisters had to pause to see if anyone else would try to come in the house. A few seconds later the kitchen window exploded. A small metal ball bounced off the wall and rolled across the floor. Pop Somethin's love of war movies gave Queenie the knowledge of what the metal ball was.

"Grenade! Run, Princess! Run!"

Queenie dropped the suitcase and Princess dropped the rifle as the sisters ran toward the living room. The grenade exploded just as they reached the front door. A split second later a second explosion rocked the house's foundation. The gas line on the stove erupted and tore the house apart. Luckily the twins were clear when it all blew up.

Gunfire sounded behind them as they ran through a neighbor's yard. Because they were in their own neck of the woods, they were able to outrun their pursuers. A few blocks later they flagged down a ride.

Chapter 20

Pop Somethin' ran his hands through his dreadlocks in frustration. He took a deep breath, closing his eyes and trying to clear his mind. Blood pulsed through his temples, the beating echoing in his ears like a steady drumbeat. When he opened his eyes again, Princess and Queenie were watching him from the couch across the room. The news they brought had crushed him, stealing his voice and tangling his thoughts.

"All the money gone?" he asked, his voice cracking.

"We tried to get it, baby, but it was too many of them," Princess said.

"They had grenades," Queenie added. "The house blew up. Everything gone."

"Fuck!" Pop cursed, slamming his hand on the table. "That was everything we had! Four hundred thousand. Gone."

No words could express the feelings shared by all three lovers. Everything they had worked hard and spilled blood for was gone, their dreams of Jamaica literally gone up in smoke. All they had was the money in their pockets, which wasn't much. A little more than a thousand dollars between the three of them. The only car they had was Pop's Maserati. The only place they had to lay their heads was C-Note's playa pad. The only clothes they had were on their backs. The only weapons they had were Pop Somethin's two Desert Eagles. One held four bullets, the other had two. An army was on their asses, and they didn't even have enough bullets to defend themselves. Now it was two in the morning and they were holed up in C-Note's playa pad trying to plan their next move.

"Yo' boy is foul, baby," Princess spoke up.

"I heard them niggas speaking in Spanish while I was in the closet. The only Latinos we connected to is Gonzo," Queenie said.

Pop exhaled loudly, unable to find the words to speak. He shook his head from side to side like he was trying to un-hear the words spoken by his women. He was so close to his goal. Saving C-Note's ass in prison had gotten him paid, and now it was all gone.

The vibrating of his phone on the table got the women's attention. Pop acted as if he didn't know someone was calling his phone. He stayed where he was, not moving to answer, so Queenie picked it up. She smirked after looking at the screen. "It's him."

That got Pop's attention. "Answer it on speaker phone."

Murder shown in Queenie's eyes as she answered. "Hello?"

"Where Pop at?" C-Note shouted.

"Right here. He can hear you."

"Pop, they burned down Lux, bruh! They burned down my shit."

Pop Somethin' just stared at the phone, not speaking.

"Pop, you hear? They burned down my club!"

The big man shook his head, staying silent, so Queenie spoke up. "Our house got burned down. All our money gone."

"What?" C-Note asked, wondering if he heard her right.

Queenie got aggressive. "All our shit gone. They blew up our house!"

It was C-Note's turn to get quiet, but it didn't last long. "Pop, say somethin'. What we gon' do?"

Everybody waited on edge, wondering if the killer would ever speak. It took a while. "Where you at?"

"On my way to get Shanice and her shorty. We gettin' the fuck outta Texas. Fuck it. I'm goin' on the run."

"Come pick me up. I wanna ride wit' you."

"I'm gettin' on the highway right now. I'm about to leave Dallas."

"Turn around and come get me. I need to be there in case these niggas try to get at my cousin."

"Damn, Pop," C-Note breathed, giving in. "I'm on my way."

"You want us to come wit' chu?" Queenie asked after hanging up the phone.

Pop was quiet for a few moments. He looked around the living room, his eyes landing on the two machetes hung as decoration on the wall. "Nah. I got it."

***

"What the fuck you got one of my machetes?" C-Note asked as Pop Somethin' climbed in the passenger seat of the black Camaro.

"I don't got that many bullets. If niggas get on our ass, I'ma cut they heads off."

"That's some real Jamaican shit, right there," C-Note chuckled.

Pop didn't laugh. Instead he pulled out his cell phone and brought a number onto the screen. He showed it to C-Note. "You know who number this is?"

"Nah. Whose is it?"

"You remember when I had to go to New Orleans to put in that work for Gonzo?"

J-BLUNT

C-Note nodded. "Yeah. You said you fucked Nurse Baccara fine ass. Is that her number?"

"Nah. This the number I called to let Gonzo know I took care of that bidness. This Marco number. Gonzo bodyguard. I'm 'bout to call him to see if he can put me in touch wit' Gonzo. If you lie to me, bruh, I'm killin' yo' sister and nephews. Did you snitch on Gonzo?"

Terror shown on C-Note's face as he took his eyes off the highway and looked at Pop Somethin'. The friend he had grown to love and trust had transformed into a monster. His eyes were red with anger, jaw clenched, lips snarled into a mug, nostrils wide and flaring.

"C'mon, Pop. You know I –"

A hard back-fist to the face made C-Note swallow his words. Blinding light flashed in his brain as his nose and lips began to bleed. The Camaro swerved as C-Note lost control. At sixty-five miles an hour on a dark highway, the end of both of their lives looked near. Fortunately for them both, Pop had quick reflexes. He grabbed the steering wheel and got control of the car. Smashing C-Note against the door, Pop Somethin' slid into the driver's seat and steered the sports car to the side of the road. After parking, he opened the door and shoved C-Note out of the car.

"Awe, man," C-Note moaned as he hit the pavement. "C'mon, Pop. Don't do me like this."

Beside the highway was woods and brush. Pop grabbed the machete and drug C-Note by the ankle into the woods. When they were far enough from the road that they couldn't be seen, Pop began ripping at C-Note's pants.

A GANGSTER'S CODE

"What the fuck you doin', bruh?" C-Note resisted, holding onto his jeans. A punch to the face made him loosen his grip.

After Pop took the pants, he used them to tie C-Note to a tree. C-Note began to cry. "C'mon, Pop. Please, bruh. Don't kill me. Please. I got money. Five hunnit Gs. It's yours. Just let me go."

Pop finally spoke up, his words harsh and accusing. "Gonzo fed us, nigga! Put us on anotha level. Showed us how bosses make moves. Fuck wrong wit' chu, nigga? We had it made."

"I know, Pop. I know," C-Note sobbed. "I'm sorry. I just wanted to be around for Shanice and the baby. I would do anything for her, bruh. I love her."

"When it rains, you s'posed to look for rainbows, nigga. You let the storm scare you, nigga. Fuck you doin' playin' wit' sharks if you can't swim? Didn't you learn that shit when we went to Mexico? You damn near got me killed. I'm broke 'cause of yo' bitch ass."

C-Note just lay there sobbing.

"Where that money at, Note? I need that."

"Let me go, bruh. I give you all that shit, just let me leave wit' Shanice."

"Nah. It don't work like that."

"C'mon, Pop. You gon' kill me if I tell you. Just let me go. You ain't gotta worry 'bout me to more. I'm gone. I'ma give Shanice the money. That's my word."

"Yo' word ain't shit, nigga. And you don't deserve to live. You a bitch. A coward. Do the right thing and gimme the money so I can take care of yo' shorty and Shanice."

"C'mon, Pop. Please, bruh. Don't kill me."

"I don't got time for this shit. Gimme the fuckin' money!" Pop exploded, pushing the machete through C-Note's stomach.

"Ah!"

"Where the money at, nigga? Gimme the money!" Pop screamed.

"C'mon, Pop. Let me live, bruh. Please. Let me live."

"Fuck you, nigga. You dead. You gon' have a shorty out here. You gon' gimme the money or not?"

C-Note could feel the life draining from his body as he looked up at Pop Somethin'. When he tried to speak, blood began spilling from his mouth. "C'mon, Pop. I just —"

Pop ripped the machete from his guts, and swung it at C- Note's head. The blade sliced through his neck, decapitating C-Note and getting stuck in the tree. C-Note's head rolled from his body into his lap, eyes and mouth wide open. His body jerked and spasmed as blood shot out of his neck like a fountain. Pop untied the pants from C-Note's arms and wrapped his head in them. Then he pulled out his phone and called Marco.

"Shooter, you got some fucking nerve calling my phone," Marco answered.

"Where Gonzo?"

"Don't act like you don't know. Don't you ever say his name again, you stinkin' nigger. Our farm in Mexico got hit. You and your boyfriend gave us to the feds. We have connections. You see what we can do. I'll kill your whole family if I have to, but you filthy niggers are dead. You hear me? Dead!"

"It wasn't me. It was him. I just found out. I wanna talk to the boss. I wanna make this shit right."

"You know how you can make this right? Tell me where you at so I can come kill you."

"I'ma do you one better. Tell me where you at so I can come to you."

The response threw Marco off momentarily. "You serious, *punta*? You want to come to me?"

"Yeah. Whatever it take to talk to the boss. I didn't do that bitch-ass shit. I ain't no snitch. I wanna talk to the boss. And I'm bringin' C-Note wit' me."

There was another pause on Marco's end of the line. "Okay. I'll play your game. I have to see if you really are as tough as you think you are. I'll send my people to get you. Tell me where you are."

To Be Continued...
A Gangster's Code 2
Coming Soon

Submission Guideline.

Submit the first three chapters of your completed manuscript to ldpsubmissions@gmail.com, subject line: Your book's title. The manuscript must be in a .doc file and sent as an attachment. Document should be in Times New Roman, double spaced and in size 12 font. Also, provide your synopsis and full contact information. If sending multiple submissions, they must each be in a separate email.

Have a story but no way to send it electronically? You can still submit to LDP/Ca$h Presents. Send in the first three chapters, written or typed, of your completed manuscript to:

LDP: Submissions Dept
Po Box 870494
Mesquite, Tx 75187

DO NOT send original manuscript. Must be a duplicate.

Provide your synopsis and a cover letter containing your full contact information.

Thanks for considering LDP and Ca$h Presents.

A GANGSTER'S CODE

Coming Soon from Lock Down Publications/Ca$h Presents

BOW DOWN TO MY GANGSTA

By **Ca$h**

TORN BETWEEN TWO

By **Coffee**

BLOOD STAINS OF A SHOTTA **III**

By **Jamaica**

WHEN THE STREETS CLAP BACK **III**

By **Jibril Williams**

STEADY MOBBIN

By **Marcellus Allen**

BLOOD OF A BOSS **V**

By **Askari**

LOYAL TO THE GAME **IV**

By **T.J. & Jelissa**

A DOPEBOY'S PRAYER **II**

By **Eddie "Wolf" Lee**

IF LOVING YOU IS WRONG… **III**

LOVE ME EVEN WHEN IT HURTS

By **Jelissa**

DAUGHTERS OF A SAVAGE **II**

By **Chris Green**

TRAPHOUSE KING **II**

By **Hood Rich**

BLAST FOR ME **II**

RAISED AS A GOON **V**

J-BLUNT

By **Ghost**
ADDICTIED TO THE DRAMA **III**
By **Jamila Mathis**
LIPSTICK KILLAH **III**
By **Mimi**
WHAT BAD BITCHES DO **II**
By **Aryanna**
THE COST OF LOYALTY **II**
By **Kweli**
SHE FELL IN LOVE WITH A REAL ONE
By **Tamara Butler**
LOVE SHOULDN'T HURT II
By **Meesha**
CORRUPTED BY A GANGSTA **II**
By **Destiny Skai**
SHE FELL IN LOVE WITH A REAL ONE II
By **Tamara Butler**
A GANGSTER'S CODE II
By **J-Blunt**

Available Now
RESTRAINING ORDER **I & II**
By **CA$H & Coffee**
LOVE KNOWS NO BOUNDARIES **I II & III**
By **Coffee**
RAISED AS A GOON I, II, III & IV
BRED BY THE SLUMS I, II, III

A GANGSTER'S CODE

BLAST FOR ME
By **Ghost**
LAY IT DOWN **I & II**
LAST OF A DYING BREED
BLOOD STAINS OF A SHOTTA I & II
By **Jamaica**
LOYAL TO THE GAME
LOYAL TO THE GAME II
LOYAL TO THE GAME III
By **TJ & Jelissa**
BLOODY COMMAS I & II
SKI MASK CARTEL I & II
By **T.J. Edwards**
IF LOVING HIM IS WRONG…I & II
By **Jelissa**
WHEN THE STREETS CLAP BACK I & II
By **Jibril Williams**
A DISTINGUISHED THUG STOLE MY HEART I II & III
LOVE SHOULDN'T HURT
By **Meesha**
PUSH IT TO THE LIMIT
By **Bre' Hayes**
BLOOD OF A BOSS **I, II, III & IV**
By **Askari**
THE STREETS BLEED MURDER **I, II & III**
THE HEART OF A GANGSTA I II& III
By **Jerry Jackson**

CUM FOR ME
CUM FOR ME 2
CUM FOR ME 3
An **LDP Erotica Collaboration**
BRIDE OF A HUSTLA **I II & II**
THE FETTI GIRLS **I, II& III**
CORRUPTED BY A GANGSTA
By **Destiny Skai**
WHEN A GOOD GIRL GOES BAD
By **Adrienne**
A GANGSTER'S REVENGE **I II III & IV**
THE BOSS MAN'S DAUGHTERS
THE BOSS MAN'S DAUGHTERS II
THE BOSSMAN'S DAUGHTERS III
THE BOSSMAN'S DAUGHTERS IV
A SAVAGE LOVE **I & II**
BAE BELONGS TO ME
A HUSTLER'S DECEIT I, II
By **Aryanna**
A KINGPIN'S AMBITON
A KINGPIN'S AMBITION **II**
I MURDER FOR THE DOUGH
By **Ambitious**
TRUE SAVAGE
TRUE SAVAGE II
TRUE SAVAGE **III**
TRUE SAVAGE **IV**

A GANGSTER'S CODE

By **Chris Green**
A DOPEBOY'S PRAYER
By **Eddie "Wolf" Lee**
THE KING CARTEL **I, II & III**
By **Frank Gresham**
THESE NIGGAS AIN'T LOYAL **I, II & III**
By **Nikki Tee**
GANGSTA SHYT **I II &III**
By **CATO**
THE ULTIMATE BETRAYAL
By **Phoenix**
BOSS'N UP **I , II & III**
By **Royal Nicole**
I LOVE YOU TO DEATH
By **Destiny J**
I RIDE FOR MY HITTA
I STILL RIDE FOR MY HITTA
By **Misty Holt**
LOVE & CHASIN' PAPER
By **Qay Crockett**
TO DIE IN VAIN
By **ASAD**
BROOKLYN HUSTLAZ
By **Boogsy Morina**
BROOKLYN ON LOCK I & II
By **Sonovia**
GANGSTA CITY

J-BLUNT

By **Teddy Duke**
A DRUG KING AND HIS DIAMOND I & II
A DOPEMAN'S RICHES
By Nicole Goosby
TRAPHOUSE KING
By **Hood Rich**
LIPSTICK KILLAH **I, II**
By **Mimi**

A GANGSTER'S CODE

BOOKS BY LDP'S CEO, CA$H

TRUST IN NO MAN
TRUST IN NO MAN 2
TRUST IN NO MAN 3
BONDED BY BLOOD
SHORTY GOT A THUG
THUGS CRY
THUGS CRY 2
THUGS CRY 3
TRUST NO BITCH
TRUST NO BITCH 2
TRUST NO BITCH 3
TIL MY CASKET DROPS
RESTRAINING ORDER
RESTRAINING ORDER 2
IN LOVE WITH A CONVICT

Coming Soon
BONDED BY BLOOD 2
BOW DOWN TO MY GANGSTA

J-BLUNT

Made in the USA
Middletown, DE
27 July 2024